I0764569

FALKLAND

EDWARD BULWER-LYTTON

WILDSIDE PRESS

www.wildsidepress.com

PREFATORY NOTE TO THE KNEBWORTH EDITION.

"FALKLAND" is the earliest of Lord Lytton's prose fictions. Published before "Pelham," it was written in the boyhood of its illustrious author. In the maturity of his manhood and the fulness of his literary popularity he withdrew it from print. In this edition of his collected works the tale re-appears. It is because the morality of it was condemned by his experienced judgment, that the author of "Falkland" deliberately omitted it from each of the numerous reprints of his novels and romances which were published in England during his lifetime.

The publishers therefore desire to state the motives which have induced them, with the consent of the author's son, to include "Falkland" in the present edition of his collected works.

In the first place, this work has been for many years, and still is, accessible to English readers in every country except England. The Continental edition of it, published by Baron Tauchnitz, has a wide circulation; and since for this reason the book cannot practically be withheld from the public, it is thought desirable that the publication of it should at least be accompanied by some record of the above-mentioned fact.

In the next place, the considerations which would naturally guide an author of established reputation in the selection of early compositions for subsequent republication, are obviously inapplicable to the preparation of a posthumous standard edition of his collected works. Those who read the tale of "Falkland" at the time of its first publication have long survived the age when character is influenced by the literature of sentiment. The readers to whom it is now presented are not Lord Lytton's contemporaries; they are his posterity. To them his works have already become classical. It is only upon the minds of the young that the works of sentiment have any appreciable moral influence. But the sentiment of each age is peculiar to itself; and the purely moral influence of sentimental fiction seldom survives the age to which it was first addressed. The youngest and most impressionable reader of such works as the "Nouvelle Helöise," "Werthe," "The Robbers," "Corinne," or "René," is not now likely to be morally influenced, for good or ill, by the perusal of those masterpieces of genius. Had Byron attained the age at which great authors most realize the responsibilities of fame and genius, he might possibly have regretted, and endeavoured to suppress, the publication of "Don Juan;" but the possession of that immortal poem is an unmixed benefit to posterity, and the loss of it would have been an irreparable misfortune.

"Falkland," although the earliest, is one of the most carefully finished of its author's compositions. All that was once turbid, heating, unwholesome in the current of sentiment which flows through this history of a guilty passion "Death's immortalizing winter" has chilled and purified. The book is now a harmless, and, it may be hoped, a not uninteresting, evidence of the precocity of its author's genius; and as such, it is here reprinted.

FALKLAND.

BOOK I.

FROM ERASMUS FALKLAND, ESQ., TO THE HON. FREDERICK MONKTON.

L——, *May* —, 1822.

You are mistaken, my dear Monkton! Your description of the gayety of "the season" gives me no emotion. You speak of pleasure; I remember no labour so wearisome: you enlarge upon its changes; no sameness appears to me so monotonous. Keep, then, your pity for those who require it. From the height of my philosophy I compassionate *you.* No one is so vain as a recluse; and your jests at my hermitship and hermitage cannot penetrate the folds of a self-conceit, which does not envy you in your suppers at D—— House, nor even in your waltzes with Eleanor ——.

It is a ruin rather than a house which I inhabit. I have not been at L—— since my return from abroad, and during those years the place has gone rapidly to decay; perhaps, for that reason, it suits me better,—*tel maître telle maison.*

Of all my possessions this is the least valuable in itself, and derives the least interest from the associations of childhood, for it was not at L—— that any part of that period was spent. I have, however, chosen it for my present retreat, because here only I am personally unknown, and therefore little likely to be disturbed. I do not, indeed, wish for the interruptions designed as civilities; I rather gather around myself, link after link, the chains that connected me with the world. I find among my own thoughts that variety and occupation which you only experience in your intercourse with others; and I make, like the Chinese, my map of the universe consist of a circle in a square, — the circle is my own empire of thought *and self;* and it is to the scanty corners which it leaves without, that I banish whatever belongs to the remainder of mankind.

About a mile from L—— is Mr. Mandeville's beautiful villa of E——, in the midst of grounds which form a delightful contrast to the savage and wild scenery by which they are surrounded. As the house is at present quite deserted, I have obtained, through the gardener, a free admittance into his domains; and I pass there whole hours, indulging, like the hero of the "Lutrin," "*une sainte oisiveté*," listening to a little noisy brook, and letting my thoughts be almost as vague and idle as the birds which wander among the trees that surround me. I could wish, indeed, that this simile were in all things correct, — that those thoughts, if as free, were also as happy as the objects of my comparison, and could, like them, after the rovings of the day, turn at evening to a resting-place, and be still. We are the dupes and the victims of our senses: while we use them to gather from external things the hoards that we store within, we cannot foresee the punishments we prepare for ourselves, — the remembrance which stings, and the hope which deceives, the passions which promise us rapture, which reward us with despair, and the thoughts which, if they constitute the healthful action, make also the feverish excitement of our minds. What sick man has not dreamed in his delirium everything that our philosophers have said?[1] But I am growing into my old habit of gloomy reflection, and it is time that I should conclude. I meant to have written you a letter as light as your own; if I have failed, it is no wonder. "Notre cœur est un instrument incomplet, — une lyre où il manque des cordes, et où nous sommes forcés de rendre les accents de la joie sur le ton consacré aux soupirs."

[1] Quid aegrotus unquam somniavit quod philosophorum aliquis non dixerit? — LACTANTIUS.

FROM THE SAME TO THE SAME.

You ask me to give you some sketch of my life, and of that *bel mondo* which wearied me so soon. Men seldom reject an opportunity to talk of themselves; and I am not unwilling to re-examine the past, to re-connect it with the present, and to gather from a consideration of each what hopes and expectations are still left to me for the future.

But my detail must be rather of thought than of action; most of those whose fate has been connected with mine are now living, and I would not, even to you, break that tacit confidence which much of my history would require. After all, you will have no loss. The actions of another may interest, but, for the most part, it is only his reflections which come home to us; for few have acted, nearly all of us have thought.

My own vanity too would be unwilling to enter upon incidents which had their origin either in folly or in error. It is true that those follies and errors have ceased, but their effects remain. With years our *faults* diminish, but our *vices* increase.

You know that my mother was Spanish, and that my father was one of that old race of which so few scions remain, who, living in a distant country, have been little influenced by the changes of fashion, and, priding themselves on the antiquity of their names, have looked with contempt upon the modern distinctions and the mushroom nobles which have sprung up to discountenance and eclipse the plainness of more venerable and solid respectability. In his youth my father had served in the army. He had known much of men and more of books; but his knowledge, instead of rooting out, had rather been engrafted on his prejudices. He was one of that class (and I say it with a private reverence, though a public regret), who, with the best intentions, have made the worst citizens, and who think it a duty to perpetuate whatever is pernicious by having learned to consider it as sacred. He was a great country gentleman, a great sportsman, and a great Tory, —

perhaps the three worst enemies which a country can have. Though beneficent to the poor, he gave but a cold reception to the rich; for he was too refined to associate with his inferiors, and too proud to like the competition of his equals. One ball and two dinners a year constituted all the aristocratic portion of our hospitality; and at the age of twelve, the noblest and youngest companions that I possessed were a large Danish dog and a wild mountain pony, as unbroken and as lawless as myself. It is only in later years that we can perceive the immeasurable importance of the early scenes and circumstances which surrounded us. It was in the loneliness of my unchecked wanderings that my early affection for my own thoughts was conceived. In the seclusion of Nature — in whatever court she presided — the education of my mind was begun; and, even at that early age, I rejoiced (like the wild hart the Grecian poet[1] has described) in the stillness of the great woods, and the solitudes unbroken by human footstep.

The first change in my life was under melancholy auspices: my father fell suddenly ill, and died; and my mother, whose very existence seemed only held in his presence, followed him in three months. I remember that, a few hours before her death, she called me to her: she reminded me that, through her, I was of Spanish extraction; that in her country I received my birth; and that, not the less for its degradation and distress, I might hereafter find in the relations which I held to it a remembrance to value, or even a duty to fulfil. On her tenderness to me at that hour, on the impression it made upon my mind, and on the keen and enduring sorrow which I felt for months after her death, it would be useless to dwell.

My uncle became my guardian. He is, you know, a member of parliament of some reputation; very sensible and very dull; very much respected by men, very much disliked by women; and inspiring all children, of either sex, with the same unmitigated aversion which he feels for them himself.

I did not remain long under his immediate care. I was soon sent to school, — that preparatory world, where the great primal principles of human nature, in the aggression of the

[1] Euripides, Bacchae, l. 874.

strong and the meanness of the weak, constitute the earliest lesson of importance that we are taught; and where the forced *primitiæ* of that less universal knowledge which is useless to the many who in after-life neglect, and bitter to the few who improve it, are the first motives for which our minds are to be broken to terror, and our hearts initiated into tears.

Bold and resolute by temper, I soon carved myself a sort of career among my associates. A hatred to all oppression, and a haughty and unyielding character, made me at once the fear and aversion of the greater powers and principalities of the school; while my agility at all boyish games, and my ready assistance or protection to every one who required it, made me proportionally popular with, and courted by, the humbler multitude of the subordinate classes. I was constantly surrounded by the most lawless and mischievous followers whom the school could afford,—all eager for my commands, and all pledged to their execution.

In good truth, I was a worthy Rowland of such a gang; though I excelled in, I cared little for, the ordinary amusements of the school: I was fonder of engaging in marauding expeditions contrary to our legislative restrictions, and I valued myself equally upon my boldness in planning our exploits, and my dexterity in eluding their discovery. But exactly in proportion as our school terms connected me with those of my own years, did our vacations unfit me for any intimate companionship but that which I already began to discover in myself.

Twice in the year, when I went home, it was to that wild and romantic part of the country where my former childhood had been spent. There, alone and unchecked, I was thrown utterly upon my own resources. I wandered by day over the rude scenes which surrounded us; and at evening I pored, with an unwearied delight, over the ancient legends which made those scenes sacred to my imagination. I grew by degrees of a more thoughtful and visionary nature. My temper imbibed the romance of my studies; and whether, in winter, basking by the large hearth of our old hall, or stretched, in the indolent voluptuousness of summer, by the rushing streams which formed the chief characteristic of the country around us, my hours were equally wasted in those dim and luxurious dreams, which constituted, perhaps, the essence of that poetry I had not the genius to embody. It was then, by that alternate restlessness of action and idleness of reflection, into which my young years were divided, that the impress of my character was stamped: that fitfulness of temper, that affection for extremes, has accompanied me through life. Hence, not only all intermediums of emotion appear to me as tame, but even the most overwrought excitation can bring neither novelty nor zest. I have, as it were, feasted upon the passions; I have made that my daily food, which, in its strength and excess, would have been poison to others; I have rendered my mind unable to enjoy the ordinary aliments of nature; and I have wasted, by a premature indulgence, my resources and my powers, till I have left my heart, without a remedy or a hope, to whatever disorders its own intemperance has engendered.

FROM THE SAME TO THE SAME.

When I left Dr. ——'s, I was sent to a private tutor in D——e. Here I continued for about two years. It was during that time that — but what *then* befell me is for no living ear! The characters of that history are engraven on my heart in letters of fire; but it is a language that none but myself have the authority to read. It is enough for the purpose of my confessions that the events of that period were connected with the first awakening of the most powerful of human passions, and that, whatever their commencement, their end was despair! and *she* — the object of that love, the only being in the world who ever possessed the secret and the spell of my nature — *her* life was the bitterness and the fever of a troubled heart, — her rest is the grave, —

> "Non la conobbe il mondo mentre l'ebbe
> Con ibill 'io, ch 'a pianger qui rimasi."

That attachment was not so much a single event, as the first link in a long chain which was coiled around my heart.

It were a tedious and bitter history, even were it permitted, to tell you of all the sins and misfortunes to which in after-life that passion was connected. I will only speak of the more hidden but general effect it had upon my mind; though, indeed, naturally inclined to a morbid and melancholy philosophy, it is more than probable, but for that occurrence, that it would never have found matter for excitement. Thrown early among mankind, I should early have imbibed their feelings, and grown like them by the influence of custom. I should not have carried within me one unceasing remembrance, which was to teach me, like Faustus, to find nothing in knowledge but its inutility, or in hope but its deceit; and to bear like him, through the blessings of youth and the allurements of pleasure, the curse and the presence of a fiend.

FROM THE SAME TO THE SAME.

It was after the first violent grief produced by that train of circumstances to which I must necessarily so darkly allude, that I began to apply with earnestness to books. Night and day I devoted myself unceasingly to study, and from this fit I was only recovered by the long and dangerous illness it produced. Alas! there is no fool like him who wishes for knowledge! It is only through woe that we are taught to reflect, and we gather the honey of worldly wisdom, not from flowers, but thorns.

"Une grande passion malheureuse est un grand moyen de sagesse." From the moment in which the buoyancy of my spirit was first broken by real anguish, the losses of the *heart* were repaired by the experience of the *mind.* I passed at once, like Melmoth, from youth to age. What were any longer to me the ordinary avocations of my contemporaries? I had exhausted years in moments, — I had wasted, like the Eastern Queen, my richest jewel in a draught. I ceased to hope, to feel, to act, to burn: such are the impulses of the young! I learned to doubt, to reason, to analyze: such are the habits of the old! From that time, if I have not avoided the pleasures of life, I have not enjoyed them. Women, wine, the society of the gay, the commune of the wise, the lonely pursuit of knowledge, the daring visions of ambition, — all have occupied me in turn, and all alike have deceived me; but, like the Widow in the story of Voltaire, I have built at last a temple to "Time the Comforter;" I have grown calm and unrepining with years; and, if I am now shrinking from men, I have derived at least this advantage from the loneliness first made habitual by regret, — that while I feel increased benevolence to others, I have learned to look for happiness only in myself.

They alone are independent of Fortune who have made themselves a separate existence from the world.

FROM THE SAME TO THE SAME.

I went to the University with a great fund of general reading, and habits of constant application. My uncle, who, having no children of his own, began to be ambitious for me, formed great expectations of my career at Oxford. I stayed there three years, and did nothing! I did not gain a single prize, nor did I attempt anything above the ordinary degree. The fact is, that nothing seemed to me worth the labour of success. I conversed with those who had obtained the highest academical reputation, and I smiled with a consciousness of superiority at the boundlessness of their vanity, and the narrowness of their views. The limits of the distinction they had gained seemed to them as wide as the most extended renown; and the little knowledge their youth had acquired only appeared to them an excuse for the ignorance and the indolence of maturer years. Was it to equal these that I was to labour? I felt that I already surpassed them! Was it to gain *their* good opinion, or, still worse, that of their admirers? Alas! I had too long learned to live for myself to find any happiness in the respect of the idlers I despised.

I left Oxford at the age of twenty-one. I succeeded to the large estates of my inheritance, and for the first time I felt the vanity so natural to youth when I went up to London to enjoy the resources of the Capital, and to display the powers

I possessed to revel in whatever those resources could yield. I found society like the Jewish temple: any one is admitted into its threshold; none but the chiefs of the institution into its recesses.

Young, rich, of an ancient and honourable name, pursuing pleasure rather as a necessary excitement than an occasional occupation, and agreeable to the associates I drew around me because my profusion contributed to their enjoyment, and my temper to their amusement, — I found myself courted by many, and avoided by none. I soon discovered that all civility is but the mask of design. I smiled at the kindness of the fathers who, hearing that I was talented, and knowing that I was rich, looked to my support in whatever political side they had espoused; I saw in the notes of the mothers their anxiety for the establishment of their daughters, and their respect for my acres; and in the cordiality of the sons who had horses to sell and rouge-et-noir debts to pay, I detected all that veneration for my money which implied such contempt for its possessor. By nature observant, and by misfortune sarcastic, I looked upon the various colourings of society with a searching and philosophic eye: I unravelled the intricacies which knit servility with arrogance, and meanness with ostentation; and I traced to its sources that universal vulgarity of inward sentiment and external manner, which, in all classes, appears to me to constitute the only unvarying characteristic of our countrymen. In proportion as I increased my knowledge of others, I shrunk with a deeper disappointment and dejection into my own resources. The first moment of real happiness which I experienced for a whole year was when I found myself about to seek, beneath the influence of other skies, that more extended acquaintance with my species which might either draw me to them with a closer connection, or at least reconcile me to the ties which already existed.

I will not dwell upon my adventures abroad: there is little to interest others in a recital which awakens no interest in one's self. I sought for wisdom, and I acquired but knowledge. I thirsted for the truth, the tenderness of love, and I found but its fever and its falsehood. Like the two Florimels of Spenser, I mistook, in my delirium, the delusive fabrication of the senses for the divine reality of the heart; and I only awoke from my deceit when the phantom I had worshipped melted into snow. Whatever I pursued partook of the energy yet fitfulness of my nature. Mingling to-day in the tumults of the city, and to-morrow alone with my own heart in the solitude of unpeopled nature; now revelling in the wildest excesses, and now tracing, with a painful and unwearied search, the intricacies of science; alternately governing others, and subdued by the tyranny which my own passions imposed, I passed through the ordeal, unshrinking yet unscathed. "The education of life," says De Staël, "perfects the thinking mind, but depraves the frivolous." I do not inquire, Monkton, to which of these classes I belong; but I feel too well, that though my mind has not been depraved, it has found no perfection but in misfortune; and that whatever be the acquirements of later years, they have nothing which can compensate for the losses of our youth.

FROM THE SAME TO THE SAME.

I returned to England. I entered again upon the theatre of its world; but I mixed now more in its greater than its lesser pursuits. I looked rather at the mass than the leaven of mankind; and while I felt aversion for the few whom I knew, I glowed with philanthropy for the crowd which I knew not.

It is in contemplating men at a distance that we become benevolent. When we mix with them, we suffer by the contact, and grow, if not malicious from the injury, at least selfish from the circumspection which our safety imposes: but when, while we feel our relationship, we are not galled by the tie; when neither jealousy nor envy nor resentment are excited, we have nothing to interfere with those more complacent and kindlier sentiments which our earliest impressions have rendered natural to our hearts. We may fly men in hatred because they have galled us, but the feeling ceases with the cause: none will willingly feed long upon bitter thoughts. It is thus that, while in the narrow circle in which we move we suffer daily from those who approach us, we can, in spite of our resentment to *them*, glow with a general benevolence to the wider relations from which we are remote; that while smarting beneath the treachery of friendship, the sting of ingratitude, the faithlessness of love, we would almost sacrifice our lives to realize some idolized theory of legislation; and that, distrustful, calculating, selfish in private, there are thousands who would, with a credulous fanaticism, fling themselves as victims before that unrecompensing Moloch which they term the Public.

Living, then, much by myself, but reflecting much upon the world, I learned to love mankind. Philanthropy brought ambition; for I was ambitious, not for my own aggrandizement, but for the service of others,—for the poor, the toiling, the degraded; these constituted that part of my fellow-beings which I the most loved, for these were bound to me by the most engaging of all human ties,—misfortune! I began to enter into the intrigues of the State; I extended my observation and inquiry from individuals to nations; I examined into the mysteries of the science which has arisen in these later days to give the lie to the wisdom of the past, to reduce into the simplicity of problems the intricacies of political knowledge, to teach us the fallacy of the system which had governed by restriction, and imagined that the happiness of nations depended upon the perpetual interference of its rulers, and to prove to us that the only unerring policy of art is to leave a free and unobstructed progress to the hidden energies and providence of Nature. But it was not only the *theoretical* investigation of the State which employed me. I mixed, though in secret, with the agents of its springs. While I seemed only intent upon pleasure, I locked in my heart the consciousness and vanity of power. In the levity of the lip I disguised the workings and the knowledge of the brain; and I looked, as with a gifted eye, upon the mysteries of the hidden depths, while I seemed to float an idler, with the herd, only on the surface of the stream.

Why was I disgusted, when I had but to put forth my hand and grasp whatever object my ambition might desire? Alas! there was in my heart always something too soft for the aims and cravings of my mind. I felt that I was wasting the young years of my life in a barren and wearisome pursuit. What to me, who had outlived vanity, would have been the admiration of the crowd? I sighed for the sympathy of *the one!* and I shrunk in sadness from the prospect of renown to ask my heart for the reality of love. For what purpose, too, had I devoted myself to the service of men? As I grew more sensible of the labour of pursuing, I saw more of the inutility of accomplishing, individual measures. There is one great and moving order of events which we may retard, but we cannot arrest, and to which, if we endeavour to hasten them, we only give a dangerous and unnatural impetus. Often, when in the fever of the midnight, I have paused from my unshared and unsoftened studies, to listen to the deadly pulsation of my heart,[1] when I have felt in its painful and tumultuous beating the very life waning and wasting within me, I have sickened to my inmost soul to remember that, amongst all those whom I was exhausting the health and enjoyment of youth to benefit, there was not one for whom my life had an interest, or by whom my death would be honoured by a tear. There is a beautiful passage in Chalmers on the want of sympathy we experience in the world. From my earliest childhood I had one deep, engrossing, yearning desire,—and that was to love and to be loved. I found, too young, the realization of that dream; it passed! and I have never known it again. The experience of long and bitter years teaches me to look with suspicion on that far recollection of the past, and to doubt if this earth could indeed produce a living form to satisfy the visions of one who has dwelt among the boyish creations of fancy,—who has shaped out in his heart an imaginary idol, arrayed it in whatever is most beautiful in nature, and breathed into the image the pure but burning spirit of that innate love from which it

1 Falkland suffered much, from very early youth, from a complaint in his heart.

sprung! It is true that my manhood has been the undeceiver of my youth, and that the meditation upon facts has disenthralled me from the visionary broodings over fiction; but what remuneration have I found in reality? If the line of the satirist be not true,—

"Souvent de tous nos maux la raison est le pire,"[1]

at least, like the madman of whom he speaks, I owe but little gratitude to the act which, "in drawing me from my error, has robbed me also of a paradise."

I am approaching the conclusion of my confessions. Men who have no ties in the world, and who have been accustomed to solitude, find, with every disappointment in the former, a greater yearning for the enjoyments which the latter can afford. Day by day I relapsed more into myself; "Man delighted me not, nor woman either." In my ambition, it was not in the means, but the end, that I was disappointed. In my friends, I complained not of treachery, but insipidity; and it was not because I was deserted, but wearied by more tender connections, that I ceased to find either excitement in seeking, or triumph in obtaining, their love. It was not, then, in a momentary disgust, but rather in the calm of satiety, that I formed that resolution of retirement which I have adopted now.

Shrinking from my kind, but too young to live wholly for myself, I have made a new tie with Nature; I have come to cement it here. I am like a bird which has wandered afar, but has returned home to its nest at last. But there is one feeling which had its origin in the world, and which accompanies me still; which consecrates my recollections of the past; which contributes to take its gloom from the solitude of the present. Do you ask me its nature, Monkton? It is my friendship for you.

FROM THE SAME TO THE SAME.

I wish that I could convey to you, dear Monkton, the faintest idea of the pleasures of indolence. You belong to that

[1] Boileau.

class which is of all the most busy, though the least active. Men of pleasure never have time for anything. No lawyer, no statesman, no bustling, hurrying, restless underling of the counter or the Exchange, is so eternally occupied as a lounger "about town." He is linked to labour by a series of undefinable nothings. His independence and idleness only serve to fetter and engross him, and his leisure seems held upon the condition of never having a moment to himself. Would that you could see me at this instant in the luxury of my summer retreat, surrounded by the trees, the waters, the wild birds, and the hum, the glow, the exultation which teem visibly and audibly through creation in the noon of a summer's day! I am undisturbed by a single intruder. I am unoccupied by a single pursuit. I suffer one moment to glide into another, without the remembrance that the next must be filled up by some laborious pleasure, or some wearisome enjoyment. It is here that I feel all the powers, and gather together all the resources, of my mind. I recall my recollections of men; and, unbiassed by the passions and prejudices which we do not experience *alone*, because their very existence depends upon others, I endeavour to perfect my knowledge of the human heart. He who would acquire that better science must arrange and analyze in private the experience he has collected in the crowd. Alas, Monkton, when you have expressed surprise at the gloom which is so habitual to my temper, did it never occur to you that my acquaintance with the world would alone be sufficient to account for it? — that knowledge is neither for the good nor the happy. Who can touch pitch, and not be defiled? Who can look upon the workings of grief and rejoice, or associate with guilt and be pure?

It has been by mingling with men, not only in their *haunts* but their *emotions*, that I have learned to know them. I have descended into the receptacles of vice; I have taken lessons from the brothel and the hell; I have watched feeling in its unguarded sallies, and drawn from the impulse of the moment conclusions which gave the lie to the previous conduct of years. But all knowledge brings us disappointment, and *this* knowledge the most; the satiety of good, the suspicion of evil, the decay of our young dreams, the premature iciness of age, the reckless, aimless, joyless indifference which follows an overwrought and feverish excitation, — *these* constitute the lot of men who have renounced *hope* in the acquisition of *thought*, and who, in learning the motives of human actions, learn only to despise the persons and the things which enchanted them like divinities before.

FROM THE SAME TO THE SAME.

I told you, dear Monkton, in my first letter, of my favourite retreat in Mr. Mandeville's grounds. I have grown so attached to it, that I spend the greater part of the day there. I am not one of those persons who always perambulate with a book in their hands, as if neither Nature nor their own reflections could afford them any rational amusement. I go there more frequently *en paresseux* than *en savant:* a small brooklet which runs through the grounds broadens at last into a deep, clear, transparent lake. Here fir and elm and oak fling their branches over the margin; and beneath their shade I pass all the hours of noon-day in the luxuries of a dreamer's revery. It is true, however, that I am never less idle than when I appear the most so. I am like Prospero in his desert island, and surround myself with spirits. A spell trembles upon the leaves; every wave comes fraught to me with its peculiar music: and an Ariel seems to whisper the secrets of every breeze, which comes to my forehead laden with the perfumes of the West. But do not think, Monkton, that it is only good spirits which haunt the recesses of my solitude. To push the metaphor to exaggeration, Memory is my Sycorax, and Gloom is the Caliban she conceives. But let me digress from myself to my less idle occupations; I have of late diverted my thoughts in some measure by a recurrence to a study to which I once was particularly devoted, — history. Have you ever remarked that people who live the most by themselves reflect the most upon others; and that he who lives surrounded by the million never thinks of any but the one individual, himself? Philosophers, moralists, historians, whose thoughts, labours, lives, have been devoted to the consideration of mankind, or the analysis of public events, have usually been remarkably attached to solitude and seclusion. We are indeed so linked to our fellow-beings, that, where we are not chained to them by action, we are carried to and connected with them by thought.

I have just quitted the observations of my favourite Bolingbroke upon history. I cannot agree with him as to its utility. The more I consider, the more I am convinced that its study has been upon the whole pernicious to mankind. It is by those details, which are always as unfair in their inference as they must evidently be doubtful in their facts, that party animosity and general prejudice are supported and sustained. There is not one abuse, one intolerance, one remnant of ancient barbarity and ignorance existing at the present day, which is not advocated, and actually confirmed, by some vague deduction from the bigotry of an illiterate chronicler, or the obscurity of an uncertain legend. It is through the constant appeal to our ancestors that we transmit wretchedness and wrong to our posterity: we should require, to corroborate an evil originating in the present day, the clearest and most satisfactory proof; but the minutest defence is sufficient for an evil handed down to us by the barbarism of antiquity. We reason from what even in old times was dubious, as if we were adducing what was certain in those in which we live. And thus we have made no sanction to abuses so powerful as history, and no enemy to the present like the past.

FROM THE LADY EMILY MANDEVILLE TO MRS. ST. JOHN.

At last, my dear Julia, I am settled in my beautiful retreat. Mrs. Dalton and Lady Margaret Leslie are all whom I could prevail upon to accompany me. Mr. Mandeville is full of the corn-laws. He is chosen chairman to a select committee in the House. He is murmuring agricultural distresses in his sleep; and when I asked him occasionally to come down here to see me, he started from a revery, and exclaimed, "Never, Mr. Speaker, as a landed proprietor, —never will I consent to my own ruin."

My boy, my own, my beautiful companion, is with me. I wish you could see how fast he can run, and how sensibly he can talk. "What a fine figure he has for his age!" said I to Mr. Mandeville the other day. "Figure! age!" said his father; "in the House of Commons he shall make a figure to every age." I know that in writing to you, you will not be contented if I do not say a great deal about myself. I shall therefore proceed to tell you that I feel already much better from the air and exercise of the journey, from the conversation of my two guests, and, above all, from the constant society of my dear boy. He was three last birthday. I think that at the age of twenty-one, I am the more childish of the two. Pray remember me to all in town who have not quite forgotten me. Beg Lady —— to send Elizabeth a subscription ticket for Almack's, and—oh, talking of Almack's, I think my boy's eyes are even more blue and beautiful than Lady C——'s.

Adieu, my dear Julia,

Ever, etc.

E. M.

Lady Emily Mandeville was the daughter of the Duke of Lindvale. She married at the age of sixteen a man of large fortune, and some parliamentary reputation. Neither in person nor in character was he much beneath or above the ordinary standard of men. He was one of Nature's Macadamized achievements. His great fault was his equality; and you longed for a hill though it were to climb, or a stone though it were in your way. Love attaches itself to something prominent, even if that something be what others would hate. One can scarcely feel extremes for mediocrity. The few years Lady Emily had been married had but little altered her character. Quick in feeling, though regulated in temper; gay, less from levity, than from that first *spring-tide* of a heart which has never yet known occasion to be sad; beautiful and pure, as an enthusiast's dream of heaven, yet bearing within the latent and powerful passion and tenderness of earth, — she mixed with all a simplicity and innocence which the extreme earliness of her marriage, and the ascetic temper of her husband, had tended less to diminish than increase. She had much of what is termed genius, — its warmth of emotion, its vividness of conception, its admiration for the grand, its affection for the good, and that dangerous contempt for whatever is mean and worthless, the very indulgence of which is an offence against the habits of the world. Her tastes were, however, too feminine and chaste ever to render her eccentric: they were rather calculated to conceal than to publish the deeper recesses of her nature; and it was beneath that polished surface of manner common to those with whom she mixed that she hid the treasures of a mine which no human eye had beheld.

Her health, naturally delicate, had lately suffered much from the dissipation of London, and it was by the advice of her physicians that she had now come to spend the summer at E——. Lady Margaret Leslie, who was old enough to be tired with the caprices of society, and Mrs. Dalton, who, having just lost her husband, was forbidden at present to partake of its amusements, had agreed to accompany her to her retreat. Neither of them was perhaps much suited to Emily's temper, but youth and spirits make almost any one congenial to us: it is from the years which confirm our habits, and the reflections which refine our taste, that it becomes easy to revolt us, and difficult to please.

On the third day after Emily's arrival at E——, she was sitting after breakfast with Lady Margaret and Mrs. Dalton. "Pray," said the former, "did you ever meet my relation, Mr. Falkland? He is in your immediate neighbourhood."

"Never; though I have a great curiosity: that fine old ruin beyond the village belongs to him, I believe."

"It does. You ought to know him; you would like him so!"

"Like him!" repeated Mrs. Dalton, who was one of those persons of *ton* who, though everything collectively, are nothing individually, — "like him? Impossible!"

"Why?" said Lady Margaret, indignantly; "he has every requisite to please, — youth, talent, fascination of manner, and great knowledge of the world."

"Well," said Mrs. Dalton, "I cannot say I discovered his perfections. He seemed to me conceited and satirical, and — and — in short, very disagreeable; *but then, to be sure, I have only seen him once.*"

"I have heard many accounts of him," said Emily, "all differing from each other; I think, however, that the generality of people rather incline to Mrs. Dalton's opinion than to yours, Lady Margaret."

"I can easily believe it. It is very seldom that he takes the trouble to please; but when he does, he is irresistible. Very little, however, is generally known respecting him. Since he came of age, he has been much abroad; and when in England, he never entered with eagerness into society. He is supposed to possess very extraordinary powers, which, added to his large fortune and ancient name, have procured him a consideration and rank rarely enjoyed by one so young. He had refused repeated offers to enter into public life; but he is very intimate with one of the ministers, who, it is said, has had the address to profit much by his abilities. All other particulars concerning him are extremely uncertain. Of his person and manners you had better judge yourself; for I am sure, Emily, that my petition for inviting him here is already granted."

"By all means," said Emily; "you cannot be more anxious to see him than I am."

And so the conversation dropped. Lady Margaret went to the library; Mrs. Dalton seated herself on the ottoman, dividing her attention between the last novel and her Italian grayhound; and Emily left the room in order to revisit her former and favourite haunts. Her young son was her companion, and she was not sorry that he was her only one. To be the instructress of an infant a mother should be its playmate; and Emily was, perhaps, wiser than she imagined when she ran with a laughing eye and a light foot over the grass, occupying herself almost with the same earnestness as her child in the same infantine amusements. As they passed the wood which led to the lake at the bottom of the grounds, the boy, who was before Emily, suddenly stopped. She came hastily up to him; and scarcely two paces before, though half hid by the steep bank of the lake beneath which he reclined, she saw a man apparently asleep. A volume of Shakspeare lay beside him; the child had seized it. As she took it from him in order to replace it, her eye rested upon the passage the boy had accidentally opened. How often in after days was that passage recalled as an omen! It was the following, —

"Ah me! for aught that ever I could read,
Could ever hear by tale or history,
The course of true love never did run smooth!"[1]

As she laid the book gently down she caught a glimpse of the countenance of the sleeper; never did she forget the expression which it wore, — stern, proud, mournful even in repose!

She did not wait for him to wake. She hurried home through the trees. All that day she was silent and abstracted; the face haunted her like a dream. Strange as it may seem, she spoke neither to Lady Margaret nor to Mrs. Dalton of her adventure. *Why?* Is there in our hearts any prescience of their misfortunes?

On the next day, Falkland, who had received and accepted Lady Margaret's invitation, was expected to dinner. Emily felt a strong yet excusable curiosity to see one of whom she had heard so many and such contradictory reports. She was alone in the saloon when he entered. At the first glance she recognized the person she had met by the lake on the day before, and she blushed deeply as she replied to his salutation. To her great relief Lady Margaret and Mrs. Dalton entered in a few minutes, and the conversation grew general.

Falkland had but little of what is called animation in manner; but his wit, though it rarely led to mirth, was sarcastic yet refined, and the vividness of his imagination

[1] Midsummer Night's Dream.

threw a brilliancy and originality over remarks which in others might have been commonplace and tame.

The conversation turned chiefly upon society; and though Lady Margaret had told her he had entered but little into its ordinary routine, Emily was struck alike by his accurate acquaintance with men, and the justice of his reflections upon manners. There also mingled with his satire an occasional melancholy of feeling, which appeared to Emily the more touching because it was always unexpected and unassumed. It was after one of these remarks, that for the first time she ventured to examine into the charm and peculiarity of the countenance of the speaker. There was spread over it that expression of mingled energy and languor, which betokens that much, whether of thought, sorrow, passion, or action, has been undergone, but resisted; has wearied, but not subdued. In the broad and noble brow, in the chiselled lip, and the melancholy depths of the calm and thoughtful eye, there sat a resolution and a power, which, though mournful, were not without their pride; which, if they had borne the worst, had also defied it. Notwithstanding his mother's country, his complexion was fair and pale; and his hair, of a light chestnut, fell in large *antique* curls over his forehead. That forehead, indeed, constituted the principal feature of his countenance. It was neither in its height nor expansion alone that its remarkable beauty consisted; but if ever thought to conceive and courage to execute high designs were embodied and visible, they were imprinted *there*.

Falkland did not stay long after dinner; but to Lady Margaret he promised all that she required of future length and frequency in his visits. When he left the room, Lady Emily went instinctively to the window to watch him depart; and all that night his low soft voice rung in her ear, like the music of an indistinct and half-remembered dream.

FROM MR. MANDEVILLE TO LADY EMILY.

Dear Emily, — Business of great importance to the country has prevented my writing to you before. I hope you have continued well since I heard from you last, and that you do all you can to preserve that retrenchment of unnecessary expenses, and observe that attention to a prudent economy, which is no less incumbent upon individuals than nations.

Thinking that you must be dull at E——, and ever anxious both to entertain and to improve you, I send you an excellent publication by Mr. Tooke,[1] together with my own two last speeches, corrected by myself.

Trusting to hear from you soon, I am, with best love to Henry

Very affectionately yours,

John Mandeville.

FROM ERASMUS FALKLAND, ESQ., TO THE HON. FREDERICK MONKTON.[2]

Well, Monkton, I have been to E——; that important event in my monastic life has been concluded. Lady Margaret was as talkative as usual; and a Mrs. Dalton, who, I find, is an acquaintance of yours, asked very tenderly after your poodle and yourself. But Lady Emily! Ay, Monkton, I know not well how to describe *her* to you. Her beauty interests not less than it dazzles. There is that deep and eloquent softness in her every word and action, which, of all charms, is the most dangerous. Yet she is rather of a playful than of the melancholy and pensive nature which generally accompanies such gentleness of manner; but there is no levity in her character, nor is that playfulness of spirit ever carried into the exhilaration of what we call "mirth." She seems, if I may use the antithesis, at once too feeling to be

[1] The Political Economist.

[2] A letter from Falkland, mentioning Lady Margaret's invitation, has been omitted.

gay, and too innocent to be sad. I remember having frequently met her husband. Cold and pompous, without anything to interest the imagination, or engage the affections, I am not able to conceive a person less congenial to his beautiful and romantic wife. But she must have been exceedingly young when she married him; and she, probably, knows not yet that she is to be pitied, because she has not yet learned that she can love.

> "Le veggio in fronte amor come in suo seggio
> Sul crin, negli occhi — su le labra amore
> Sol d'intorno al suo cuore amor non veggio."

I have been twice to her house since my first admission there. I love to listen to that soft and enchanting voice, and to escape from the gloom of my own reflections to the brightness, yet simplicity, of hers. In my earlier days this comfort would have been attended with danger; but we grow callous from the excess of feeling. We cannot re-illumine ashes. I can gaze upon her dream-like beauty, and not experience a single desire which can sully the purity of my worship. I listen to her voice when it melts in endearment over her birds, her flowers, or, in a deeper devotion, over her child; but my heart does not thrill at the tenderness of the sound. I touch her hand, and the pulses of my own are as calm as before. Satiety of the past is our best safeguard from the temptations of the future; and the perils of youth are over when it has acquired that dulness and apathy of affection which should belong only to the insensibility of age.

Such were Falkland's opinions at the time he wrote. Ah! what is so delusive as our affections? Our security is our danger,— our defiance our defeat! Day after day he went to E——. He passed the mornings in making excursions with Emily over that wild and romantic country by which they were surrounded; and in the dangerous but delicious stillness of the summer twilights, they listened to the first whispers of their hearts.

In his relationship to Lady Margaret, Falkland found his excuse for the frequency of his visits; and even Mrs. Dalton was so charmed with the fascination of his manner, that (in spite of her previous dislike) she forgot to inquire how far his intimacy at E—— was at variance with the proprieties of the world she worshipped, or in what proportion it was connected with herself.

It is needless for me to trace through all its windings the formation of that affection, the subsequent records of which I am about to relate. What is so unearthly, so beautiful, as the first birth of a woman's love? The air of heaven is not purer in its wanderings, its sunshine not more holy in its warmth. Oh! why should it deteriorate in its nature even while it increases in its degree? Why should the step which *prints, sully* also the snow? How often, when Falkland met that guiltless yet thrilling eye, which revealed to him those internal secrets that Emily was yet awhile too happy to discover; when, like a fountain among flowers, the goodness of her heart flowed over the softness of her manner to those around her, and the benevolence of her actions to those beneath,—how often he turned away with a veneration too deep for the selfishness of human passion, and a tenderness too sacred for its desires! It was in this temper (the earliest and the most fruitless prognostic of real love) that the following letter was written:—

FROM ERASMUS FALKLAND, ESQ., TO THE HON. FREDERICK MONKTON.

I have had two or three admonitory letters from my uncle.

"The summer [he says] is advancing, yet you remain stationary in your indolence. There is still a great part of Europe which you have not seen; and since you will neither enter society for a wife, nor the House of Commons for fame, spend your life, at least while it is yet free and unshackled, in those active pursuits which will render idleness hereafter more sweet; or in that observation and enjoyment among others, which will increase your resources in yourself."

All this sounds well; but I have already acquired more knowledge than will be of use either to others or myself, and

I am not willing to lose *tranquillity* here for the chance of obtaining *pleasure* elsewhere. Pleasure is indeed a holiday sensation which does not occur in ordinary life. We lose the peace of years when we hunt after the rapture of moments.

I do not know if you ever felt that existence was ebbing away without being put to its full value; as for me, I am never conscious of life without being also conscious that it is not enjoyed to the utmost. This is a bitter feeling, and its worst bitterness is our ignorance how to remove it. My indolence I neither seek nor wish to defend, yet it is rather from necessity than choice: it seems to me that there is nothing in the world to arouse me. I only ask for action, but I can find no motive sufficient to excite it. Let me then, in my indolence, not, like the world, be idle, yet dependent on others, but at least dignify the failing by some appearance of that freedom which retirement only can bestow.

My seclusion is no longer solitude; yet I do not value it the less. I spend a great portion of my time at E——. Loneliness is attractive to men of reflection, not so much because they like their own thoughts, as because they dislike the thoughts of others. Solitude ceases to charm the moment we can find a single being whose ideas are more agreeable to us than our own. I have not, I think, yet described to you the person of Lady Emily. She is tall, and slightly, yet beautifully, formed. The ill health which obliged her to leave London for E—— in the height of the season, has given her cheek a more delicate hue than I should think it naturally wore. Her eyes are light, but their lashes are long and dark; her hair is black and luxuriant, and worn in a fashion peculiar to herself; but her manners, Monkton! how can I convey to you their fascination? So simple, and therefore so faultless, so modest, and yet so tender, she seems, in acquiring the intelligence of the woman, to have only perfected the purity of the child; and now, after all that I have said, I am only more deeply sensible of the truth of Bacon's observation, that "the best part of beauty is that which no picture can express." I am loth to finish this description, because it seems to me scarcely begun; I am unwilling to continue it, because every word seems to show me more clearly those recesses of my heart, which I would have hidden even from myself. I do not *yet* love, it is true, for the time is past when I was lightly moved to passion; but I will not incur that danger, the probability of which I am seer enough to foresee. Never shall that pure and innocent heart be sullied by one who would die to shield it from the lightest misfortune. I find in myself a powerful seconder to my uncle's wishes. I shall be in London next week; till then, farewell.

E. F.

When the proverb said that "Jove laughs at lovers' vows," it meant not (as in the ordinary construction) a sarcasm on their insincerity, but *inconsistency*. We deceive others far less than we deceive ourselves. What to Falkland were resolutions which a word, a glance, could overthrow? In the world he might have dissipated his thoughts: in loneliness he concentred them; for the passions are like the sounds of Nature, only heard in her solitude. He lulled his soul to the reproaches of his conscience; he surrendered himself to the intoxication of so golden a dream; and amidst those beautiful scenes there arose, as an offering to the summer heaven, the incense of two hearts which had, through those very fires so guilty in themselves, purified and ennobled every other emotion they had conceived.

' God made the country, and man made the town,"

says the hackneyed quotation; and the feelings awakened in each differ with the genius of the place. Who can compare the frittered and divided affections formed in cities with that which crowds cannot distract by opposing temptations, or dissipation infect with its frivolities?

I have often thought that had the execution of Atala equalled its design, no human work could have surpassed it in its grandeur. What picture is more simple, though more sublime, than the vast solitude of an unpeopled wilderness, the woods, the mountains, the face of Nature, cast in the fresh yet giant mould of a new and unpolluted world; and, amidst those most silent and mighty temples of THE GREAT GOD, the lone spirit of Love reigning and brightening over all?

BOOK II.

IT is dangerous for women, however wise it be for men, "to commune with their own hearts, and to be still!" Continuing to pursue the follies of the world had been to Emily more prudent than to fly them; to pause, to separate herself from the herd, was to discover, to feel, to murmur at the vacuum of her being; and to occupy it with the feelings which it craved could in her be but the hoarding a provision for despair.

Married, before she had begun the bitter knowledge of *herself*, to a man whom it was impossible to love, yet deriving from nature a tenderness of soul which shed itself over everything around, her only escape from misery had been in the dormancy of feeling. The birth of her son had opened to her a new field of sensations, and she drew the best charm of her own existence from the life she had given to another. Had she not met Falkland, all the deeper sources of affection would have flowed into one only and legitimate channel; but those whom *he* wished to fascinate had never resisted his power, and the attachment he inspired was in proportion to the strength and ardour of his own nature.

It was not for Emily Mandeville to love such as Falkland without feeling that from that moment a separate and selfish existence had ceased *to be*. Our senses may captivate us with beauty; but in absence we forget, or by reason we can conquer, so superficial an impression. Our vanity may enamour us with rank; but the affections of vanity are traced in sand. But who can love *Genius*, and not feel that the sentiments it excites partake of its own intenseness and its own immortality? It arouses, concentrates, engrosses all our emotions, even to the most subtle and concealed. Love what is common, and ordinary objects can replace or destroy a sentiment which an ordinary object has awakened. Love what we shall not meet again amidst the littleness and insipidity which surround us, and where can we turn for a new object to replace that which has no parallel upon earth? The recovery from such a delirium is like return from a fairy-land; and still fresh in the recollections of a bright and immortal clime, how can we endure the dulness of that human existence to which for the future we are condemned?

It was some weeks since Emily had written to Mrs. St. John; and her last letter, in mentioning Falkland, had spoken of him with a reserve which rather alarmed than deceived her friend. Mrs. St. John had indeed a strong and secret reason for fear. Falkland had been the object of her own and her earliest attachment, and she knew well the singular and mysterious power which he exercised at will over the mind. He had, it is true, never returned, nor even known of, her feelings towards him; and during the years which had elapsed since she last saw him, and in the new scenes which her marriage with Mr. St. John had opened, she had almost forgotten her early attachment, when Lady Emily's letter renewed its remembrance. She wrote in answer an impassioned and affectionate caution to her friend. She spoke much (after complaining of Emily's late silence) in condemnation of the character of Falkland, and in warning of its fascinations; and she attempted to arouse alike the virtue and the pride which so often triumph in alliance, when separately they would so easily fail. In this Mrs. St. John probably imagined she was actuated solely by friendship; but in the best actions there is always some latent evil in the motive; and the selfishness of a jealousy, though hopeless not conquered, perhaps predominated over the less interested feelings which were all that she acknowledged to herself.

In this work it has been my object to portray the progress of the passions; to chronicle a history rather by thoughts and feelings than by incidents and events; and to lay open those minuter and more subtle mazes and secrets of the human heart, which in modern writings have been so sparingly exposed. It is with this view that I have from time to time broken the thread of narration, in order to bring forward more vividly the characters it contains; and in laying no claim to the ordinary ambition of tale-writers, I have deemed myself at liberty to deviate from the ordinary courses they pursue. Hence the motive and the excuse for the insertion of the following extracts, and of occasional letters. They portray the interior struggle when Narration would look only to the external event, and trace the lightning "home to its cloud," when History would only mark the spot where it scorched or destroyed.

EXTRACTS FROM THE JOURNAL OF LADY EMILY MANDEVILLE.

Tuesday.— More than seven years have passed since I began this journal! I have just been looking over it from the commencement. Many and various are the feelings which it attempts to describe,— anger, pique, joy, sorrow, hope, pleasure, weariness, *ennui;* but never, never once, humiliation or remorse! — these were not doomed to be my portion in the bright years of my earliest youth. How shall I describe them now? I have received — I have read, as well as my tears would let me — a long letter from Julia. It is true that I have not dared to write to her: when sha l I answer this? She has shown me the state of my heart; I more than suspected it before. Could I have dreamed two months — six weeks — since that I should have a single feeling of which I could be ashamed? *He* has just been here,— *he*, the only one in the world, for all the world seems concentred in him. He observed my distress, for I looked on him; and my lips quivered and my eyes were full of tears. He came to me, he sat next to me, he whispered his interest, his anxiety — and was this all? Have I loved before I even knew that I was beloved? No, no; the tongue was silent, but the eye, the cheek, the manner — alas! *these* have been but too eloquent!

Wednesday. — It was so sweet to listen to his low and tender voice; to watch the expression of his countenance,— even to breathe the air that he inhaled. But now that I know its cause, I feel that this pleasure is a crime, and I am miserable even when he is with me. He has not been here to-day. It is past three. Will he come? I rise from my seat; I go to the window for breath; I am restless, agitated, disturbed. Lady Margaret speaks to me,— I scarcely answer her. My boy — yes, my dear, dear Henry comes, and I feel that I am again a mother. Never will I betray that duty, though I have forgotten one as sacred, though less dear! Never shall my son have cause to blush for his parent! I will fly hence,— I will see *him* no more!

FROM ERASMUS FALKLAND, ESQ., TO THE HON. FREDERICK MONKTON.

Write to me, Monkton,— exhort me, admonish me, or forsake me forever. I am happy, yet wretched; I wander in the delirium of a fatal fever, in which I see dreams of a brighter life, but every one of them only brings me nearer to death. Day after day I have lingered here, until weeks have flown — and for what? Emily is not like the women of the world; virtue, honour, faith, are not to her the mere *convenances* of society. "There is no crime," said Lady A., "where there is concealment." Such can never be the creed of Emily Mandeville. She will not disguise guilt either in the levity of the world or in the affectations of sentiment. She will be wretched, and forever. *I* hold the destinies of her future life, and yet I am base enough to hesitate whether to save or destroy her. Oh, how fearful, how selfish, how degrading is unlawful love!

You know my theoretical benevolence for everything that lives; you have often smiled at its vanity. I see now that you were right; for it seems to me almost superhuman virtue not to destroy the person who is dearest to me on earth.

I remember writing to you some weeks since that I would come to London. Little did I know of the weakness of my own mind. I told her that I intended to depart. She turned pale, she trembled; but she did not speak. Those signs which should have hastened my departure have taken away the strength even to think of it.

I am here still! I go to E—— every day. Sometimes we sit in silence; I dare not trust myself to speak. How dangerous are such moments! "Ammutiscon lingue parlen l'alme."

Yesterday they left us alone. We had been conversing with Lady Margaret on indifferent subjects. There was a pause for some minutes. I looked up; Lady Margaret had left the room. The blood rushed into my cheek; my eyes met Emily's; I would have given worlds to have repeated with my lips what those eyes expressed. I could not even speak,—I felt choked with contending emotions. There was not a breath stirring; I heard my very heart beat. A thunderbolt would have been a relief. O God! if there be a curse, it is to burn, swell, madden with feelings which you are doomed to conceal! This is, indeed, to be "a cannibal of one's own heart."[1]

It was sunset. Emily was alone upon the lawn which sloped towards the lake, and the blue still waters beneath broke, at bright intervals, through the scattered and illuminated trees. She stood watching the sun sink with wistful and tearful eyes. Her soul was sad within her. The ivy which love first wreathes around his work had already faded away, and she now only saw the desolation of the ruin it concealed. Never more for her was that freshness of unawakened feeling which invests all things with a perpetual daybreak of sunshine and incense and dew. The heart may survive the decay or rupture of an innocent and lawful affection,—"la marque reste, mais la blessure guérit,"—but the love of darkness and guilt is branded in a character ineffaceable, eternal! The one is, like lightning, more likely to dazzle than to destroy, and, divine even in its danger, it *makes holy what it sears;*[2] but the other is like that sure and

[1] Bacon.   [2] According to the ancient superstition.

deadly fire which fell upon the cities of old, graving in the barrenness of the desert it had wrought the record and perpetuation of a curse. A low and thrilling voice stole upon Emily's ear. She turned,— Falkland stood beside her.

"I felt restless and unhappy," he said, "and I came to seek you. If (writes one of the fathers) a guilty and wretched man could behold, though only for a few minutes, the countenance of an angel, the calm and glory which it wears would so sink into his heart, that he would pass at once over the gulf of gone years into his first unsullied state of purity and hope; perhaps I thought of that sentence when I came to you."

"I know not," said Emily, with a deep blush at this address, which formed her only answer to the compliment it conveyed,—"I know not why it is, but to me there is always something melancholy in this hour,— something mournful in seeing the beautiful day die with all its pomp and music, its sunshine, and songs of birds."

"And yet," replied Falkland, "if I remember the time when my feelings were more in unison with yours (for at present external objects have lost for me much of their influence and attraction), the melancholy you perceive has in it a vague and ineffable sweetness not to be exchanged for more exhilarated spirits. The melancholy which arises from no cause within ourselves is like music,— it enchants us in proportion to its effect upon our feelings. Perhaps its chief charm (though this it requires the contamination of after years before we can fathom and define) is in the purity of the sources it springs from. Our feelings can be but little sullied and worn while they can yet respond to the passionless and primal sympathies of Nature; and the sadness you speak of is so void of bitterness, so allied to the best and most delicious sensations we enjoy, that I should imagine the *very happiness of heaven partook rather of melancholy than mirth.*"

There was a pause of some moments. It was rarely that Falkland alluded even so slightly to the futurity of another world; and when he did, it was never in a careless and commonplace manner, but in a tone which sank deep into Emily's heart. "Look," she said, at length, "at that beautiful star, — the first and brightest! I have often thought it was like the promise of life beyond the tomb,— a pledge to us that, even in the depths of midnight, the earth shall have a light, unquenched and unquenchable, from Heaven!"

Emily turned to Falkland as she said this, and her countenance sparkled with the enthusiasm she felt. But *his* face was deadly pale. There went over it, like a cloud, an expression of changeful and unutterable thought; and then, passing suddenly away, it left his features calm and bright in all their noble and intellectual beauty. Her soul yearned to him, as she looked, with the tenderness of a sister.

They walked slowly towards the house. "I have frequently," said Emily, with some hesitation, "been surprised at the little enthusiasm you appear to possess even upon subjects where your conviction must be strong."

"*I have thought enthusiasm away!*" replied Falkland; "it was the loss of hope which brought me reflection, and in reflection I forgot to feel. Would that I had not found it so easy to recall what I thought I had lost forever!"

Falkland's cheek changed as he said this, and Emily sighed faintly, for she felt his meaning. In him that allusion to his love had aroused a whole train of dangerous recollections; for Passion is the avalanche of the human heart,— *a single breath can dissolve it from its repose.*

They remained silent; for Falkland would not trust himself to speak, till, when they reached the house, he faltered out his excuses for not entering, and departed. He turned towards his solitary home. The grounds at E—— had been laid out in a classical and costly manner, which contrasted forcibly with the wild and simple nature of the surrounding scenery. Even the short distance between Mr. Mandeville's house and L—— wrought as distinct a change in the character of the country as any length of space could have effected. Falkland's ancient and ruinous abode, with its shattered arches and moss-grown parapets, was situated on a gentle declivity, and surrounded by dark elm and larch trees. It still retained some traces both of its former consequence, and of the perils to which that consequence had exposed it. A broad ditch, overgrown with weeds, indicated the remains of what once had been a moat; and huge rough stones, scattered around it, spoke of the outworks the fortification had anciently possessed, and the stout resistance they had made in "the Parliament Wars" to the sturdy followers of Ireton and Fairfax. The moon, that flatterer of decay, shed its rich and softening beauty over a spot which else had, indeed, been desolate and cheerless, and kissed into light the long and unwaving herbage which rose at intervals from the ruins, like the false parasites of fallen greatness. But for Falkland the scene had no interest or charm, and he turned with a careless and unheeding eye to his customary apartment. It was the only one in the house furnished with luxury, or even comfort. Large bookcases, inlaid with curious carvings in ivory; busts of the few public characters the world had ever produced worthy, in Falkland's estimation, of the homage of posterity; elaborately-wrought hangings from Flemish looms; and French *fauteuils* and sofas of rich damask, and massy gilding (relics of the magnificent days of Louis Quatorze), bespoke a costliness of design suited rather to Falkland's wealth than to the ordinary simplicity of his tastes.

A large writing-table was overspread with books in various languages, and upon the most opposite subjects. Letters and papers were scattered amongst them; Falkland turned carelessly over the latter. One of the epistolary communications was from Lord ——, the ——. He smiled bitterly, as he read the exaggerated compliments it contained, and saw to the bottom of the shallow artifice they were meant to conceal. He tossed the letter from him, and opened the scattered volumes, one after another, with that languid and sated feeling common to all men who have read deeply enough to feel how much they have learned, and how little they know.

"We pass our lives," thought he, "in sowing what we are never to reap! We endeavour to erect a tower, which shall reach the heavens, in order to escape *one* curse, and lo! we are smitten by *another!* We would soar from a common evil, and from that moment *we are divided by a separate language from our race!* Learning, science, philosophy, the world of men and of imagination, I ransacked — and for what? I centred my happiness in wisdom. I looked upon the aims of others with a scornful and loathing eye. I held commune with those who have gone before me; I dwelt among the monuments of their minds, and made their records familiar to me as friends; I penetrated the womb of nature, and went with the secret elements to their home; I arraigned the stars before me, and learned the method and the mystery of their courses; I asked the tempest its bourn, and questioned the winds of their path. This was not sufficient to satisfy my thirst for knowledge, and I searched in this lower world for new sources to content it. Unseen and unsuspected, I saw and agitated the springs of the automaton that we call 'the Mind.' I found a clew for the labyrinth of human motives, and I surveyed the hearts of those around me as through a glass. Vanity of vanities! What have I acquired? I have separated myself from my kind, but not from those worst enemies, my passions! I have made a solitude of my soul, but I have not mocked it with the appellation of Peace.[1] In flying the herd, I have not escaped from myself; like the wounded deer, the barb was within me, and *that* I could not fly!"

With these thoughts he turned from his revery, and once more endeavoured to charm his own reflections by those which ought to speak to us of quiet, for they are graven on the pages of the dead; but his attempts were as idle as before. His thoughts were still wandering and confused, and could neither be quieted nor collected; he read, but he scarcely distinguished one page from another; he wrote, — the ideas refused to flow at his call; and the only effort at connecting his feelings which even partially succeeded, was in the verses which I am about to place before the reader. It is a common property of poetry, however imperfectly the gift be possessed, to speak to the hearts of others in proportion as the sentiments it would express are felt in our own; and I subjoin the lines which bear the date of that evening, in the

[1] Solitudinem faciunt, pacem appellant. — TACITUS.
They make a solitude, and call it peace. — BYRON.

hope that, more than many pages, they will show the morbid yet original character of the writer, and the particular sources of feeling from which they took the bitterness that pervades them.

KNOWLEDGE.

Ergo hominum genus incassum frustraque laborat
Semper, et in curis consumit inanibus aevum. — LUCRETIUS.

'T is midnight! Round the lamp which o'er
My chamber sheds its lonely beam,
Is wisely spread the varied lore
Which feeds in youth our feverish dream, —

The dream, the thirst, the wild desire,
Delirious yet divine, to *know;*
Around to roam, above aspire,
And drink the breath of Heaven below!

From Ocean, Earth, the Stars, the Sky,
To lift mysterious Nature's pall;
And bare before the kindling eye
In MAN the darkest mist of all!

Alas! what boots the midnight oil?
The madness of the struggling mind?
Oh, vague the hope, and vain the toil,
Which only leave us doubly blind!

What learn we from the Past? — the same
Dull course of glory, guilt, and gloom:
I asked the Future, and there came
No voice from its unfathomed womb.

The Sun was silent, and the wave;
The air but answered with its breath;
But Earth was kind; and from the grave
Arose the eternal answer, — *Death!*

And *this* was all! We need no sage
To teach us Nature's only truth!
O fools! o'er Wisdom's idle page
To waste the hours of golden youth!

In Science wildly do we seek
What only withering years should bring, —
The languid pulse, the feverish cheek,
The spirits drooping on their wing!

To think — is but to learn to groan;
  To scorn what all beside adore;
To feel amid the world alone,
  An alien on a desert shore;

To lose the only ties which seem
  To idler gaze in mercy given!
To find love, faith, and hope, a dream,
  And turn to dark despair from heaven!

. . . .

I pass on to a wilder period of my history. The passion, as yet only revealed by the eye, was now to be recorded by the lip; and the scene which witnessed the first confession of the lovers was worthy of the last conclusion of their loves!

E—— was about twelve miles from a celebrated cliff on the seashore, and Lady Margaret had long proposed an excursion to a spot curious alike for its natural scenery and the legends attached to it. A day was at length fixed for accomplishing this plan. Falkland was of the party. In searching for something in the pockets of the carriage, his hand met Emily's, and involuntarily pressed it. She withdrew it hastily, but he felt it tremble. He did not dare to look up: that single contact had given him a new life; intoxicated with the most delicious sensations, he leaned back in silence. A fever had entered his veins, the thrill of the touch had gone like fire into his system, all his frame seemed one nerve.

Lady Margaret talked of the weather and the prospect, wondered how far they had got, and animadverted on the roads, till at last, like a child, she talked herself to rest. Mrs. Dalton read "Guy Mannering;" but neither Emily nor her lover had any occupation or thought in common with their companions: silent and absorbed, they were only alive to the vivid existence of the present. Constantly engaged, as we are, in looking behind us or before, if there be one hour in which we feel only the time being, — in which we feel sensibly that we live, and that those moments of the present are full of the enjoyment, the rapture of existence, — it is when we are with the *one* person whose life and spirits have become the great part and principle of our own. They reached their destination,—a small inn close by the shore. They rested there a short time, and then strolled along the sands towards the cliff. Since Falkland had known Emily, her character was much altered. Six weeks before the time I write of, and in playfulness and lightness of spirits she was almost a child; now those indications of an unawakened heart had mellowed into a tenderness full of that melancholy so touching and holy, even amid the voluptuous softness which it breathes and inspires. But this day, whether from that coquetry so common to all women, or from some cause more natural to *her*, she seemed gayer than Falkland ever remembered to have seen her. She ran over the sands, picking up shells, and tempting the waves with her small and fairy feet, not daring to look at him, and yet speaking to him at times with a quick tone of levity which hurt and offended him, even though he knew the depth of those feelings she could not disguise either from him or from herself. By degrees his answers and remarks grew cold and sarcastic. Emily affected pique; and when it was discovered that the cliff was still nearly two miles off, she refused to proceed any farther. Lady Margaret talked her at last into consent, and they walked on as sullenly as an English party of pleasure possibly could do, till they were within three quarters of a mile of the place, when Emily declared she was so tired that she really could not go on. Falkland looked at her, perhaps, with no very amiable expression of countenance, when he perceived that she seemed really pale and fatigued; and when she caught his eyes, tears rushed into her own.

"Indeed, indeed, Mr. Falkland," said she, eagerly, "this is *not* affectation. I am very tired; but rather than prevent your amusement, I will endeavour to go on."

"Nonsense, child," said Lady Margaret, "you *do* seem tired. Mrs. Dalton and Falkland shall go to the rock, and I will stay here with you." This proposition, however, Lady Emily (who knew Lady Margaret's wish to see the rock) would not hear of; she insisted upon staying by herself. "Nobody will run away with me; and I can very easily amuse myself with picking up shells till you come back."

After a long remonstrance, which produced no effect, this plan was at last acceded to. With great reluctance Falkland set off with his two companions; but after the first step, he turned to look back. He caught her eye, and felt from that moment that their reconciliation was sealed. They arrived at last at the cliff. Its height, its excavations, the romantic interest which the traditions respecting it had inspired, fully repaid the two women for the fatigue of their walk. As for Falkland, he was unconscious of everything around him; he was full of "sweet and bitter thoughts." In vain the man whom they found loitering there, in order to serve as a guide, kept dinning in his ear stories of the marvellous, and exclamations of the sublime. The first words which aroused him were these: "It 's lucky, please your Honour, that you have just saved the tide. It is but last week that three poor people were drowned in attempting to come here; as it is, you will have to go home round the cliff." Falkland started: he felt his heart stand still. "Good God!" cried Lady Margaret, "what will become of Emily?"

They were at that instant in one of the caverns, where they had already been loitering too long. Falkland rushed out to the sands. The tide was hurrying in with a deep sound, which came on his soul like a knell. He looked back towards the way they had come: not one hundred yards distant, and the waters had already covered the path! An eternity would scarcely atone for the horror of that moment! One great characteristic of Falkland was his presence of mind. He turned to the man who stood beside him,—he gave him a cool and exact description of the spot where he had left Emily. He told him to repair with all possible speed to his home, to launch his boat, to row it to the place he had described. "Be quick," he added, "and you *must* be in time; if you are, you shall never know poverty again."

The next moment he was already several yards from the spot. He ran, or rather flew, till he was stopped by the waters. He rushed in; they were over a hollow between two rocks,—they were already up to his chest. "There is yet hope," thought he, when he had passed the spot, and saw the smooth sand before him. For some minutes he was scarcely sensible of existence; and then he found himself breathless at *her* feet. Beyond, towards T—— (the small inn I spoke of), the waves had already reached the foot of the rocks, and precluded all hope of return. Their only chance was the possibility that the waters had not yet rendered impassable the hollow through which Falkland had just waded. He scarcely spoke; at least he was totally unconscious of what he said. He hurried her on breathless and trembling, with the sound of the booming waters ringing in his ear, and their billows advancing to his very feet. They arrived at the hollow: a single glance sufficed to show him that their solitary hope was past! The waters, before up to his chest, had swelled considerably; he could not swim. He saw in that instant that they were girt with a hastening and terrible death. Can it be believed that with that certainty ceased his fear? He looked in the pale but calm countenance of her who clung to him, and a strange tranquillity, even mingled with joy, possessed him. Her breath was on his cheek, her form was reclining on his own, his hand clasped hers; if they were to die, it was thus. What could life afford to him more dear?

"It is in this moment," said he, and he knelt as he spoke, "that I dare tell you what otherwise my lips never should have revealed. I love, — I adore you! Turn not away from me thus. In life our persons were severed; if our hearts are united in death, then death will be sweet." She turned,— *her cheek was no longer pale!* He rose,— he clasped her to his bosom; his lips pressed hers. Oh! that long, deep, burning pressure! — youth, love, life, soul,— all concentrated in that one kiss! Yet the same cause which occasioned the avowal hallowed also the madness of his heart. What had the passion, declared only at the approach of death, with the more earthly desires of life? They looked to heaven,— it was calm and unclouded; the evening lay there in its balm and perfume, and the air was less agitated than their sighs. They turned towards the beautiful sea which was to be their grave: the wild birds flew over it exultingly; the far vessels seemed "rejoicing to run their course." All was full of the breath, the glory, the life of nature; and in how many minutes was all to be as *nothing!* Their existence would resemble the ships that have gone down at sea in the very smile of the element that destroyed them. They looked into each other's eyes, and they drew still nearer together. Their hearts, in safety apart, mingled in peril and became one. Minutes rolled on, and the great waves came dashing round them. They stood on the loftiest eminence they could reach. The spray broke over their feet: the billows rose — rose; they were speechless. He thought he heard her heart beat, but her lip trembled not. A speck! a boat! "Look up, Emily! look up! See how it cuts the waters. Nearer, nearer! but a little longer, and we are safe. It is but a few yards off! it approaches! it touches the rock!" Ah! what to them henceforth was the value of life, when the moment of discovering its charm became also the date of its misfortunes, and when the death they had escaped was the only method of cementing their union without consummating their guilt?

FROM ERASMUS FALKLAND, ESQ., TO THE HON FREDERICK MONKTON.

I will write to you at length to-morrow. Events have occurred to alter, perhaps, the whole complexion of the future. I am now going to Emily to propose to her to fly. We are not *les gens du monde,* who are ruined by the loss of public opinion. She has felt that I can be to her far more than the world; and as for me, what would I not forfeit for one touch of her hand?

EXTRACTS FROM THE JOURNAL OF LADY EMILY MANDEVILLE.

Friday. — Since I wrote yesterday in these pages the narrative of our escape, I have done nothing but think over those moments, too dangerous because too dear; but at last I have steeled my heart. I have yielded to my own weakness too long; I shudder at the abyss from which I have escaped. I can yet fly. He will come here to-day, — he shall receive my farewell.

Saturday morning, four o'clock. — I have sat in this room alone since eleven o'clock. I cannot give vent to my feelings; they seem as if crushed by some load from which it is impossible to rise. "*He is gone, and forever!*" I sit repeating those words to myself, scarcely conscious of their meaning. Alas! when to-morrow comes, and the next day, and the next, and yet I see him not, I shall awaken, indeed, to all the agony of my loss! He came here, he saw me alone, he implored me to fly. I did not dare to meet his eyes; I hardened my heart against his voice. I knew the part I was to take, — I have adopted it; but what struggles, what misery, has it not occasioned me! Who could have thought it had been so hard to be virtuous! His eloquence drove me from one defence to another, and then I had none but *his* mercy. I opened my heart; I showed him its weakness, I implored his forbearance. My tears, my anguish, convinced him of my sincerity. We have parted in bitterness, but, thank Heaven, not in guilt! He has entreated permission to write to me. How could I refuse him? Yet I may not — cannot — write to him again! How *could* I, indeed, suffer my heart to pour forth one of its feelings in reply, for would there be one word of regret, or one term of endearment, which my inmost soul would not echo?

Sunday. —Yes, *that day* — but I must not think of this; my very religion I dare not indulge. O God! how wretched I am! His visit was always the great era in the day; it employed all my hopes till he came, and all *my memory* when he was gone. I sit now and look at the place he used to fill, till I feel the tears rolling silently down my cheek; they come without an effort, they depart without relief.

Monday. — Henry asked me where Mr. Falkland was gone; I stooped down to hide my confusion. When shall I hear from him? To-morrow? Oh that it were come! I have placed the clock before me, and I actually count the minutes. He left a book here; it is a volume of "Melmoth." I have read over every word of it, and whenever I have come to a pencil-mark by him, I have paused to dream over that varying and eloquent countenance, the low soft tone of that tender voice, till the book has fallen from my hands, and I have started to find the utterness of my desolation!

FROM ERASMUS FALKLAND, ESQ., TO LADY EMILY MANDEVILLE.

—— Hotel, London.

For the first time in my life I write to you! How my hand trembles! how my cheek flushes! A thousand, thousand thoughts rush upon me, and almost suffocate me with the variety and confusion of the emotions they awaken! I am agitated alike with the rapture of writing to you, and with the impossibility of expressing the feelings which I cannot distinctly unravel even to myself. You love me, Emily, and yet I have fled from you, and at your command; but the thought that, though absent, I am not forgotten, supports me through all.

It was with a feverish sense of weariness and pain that I found myself entering this vast reservoir of human vices. I became at once sensible of the sterility of that polluted soil so incapable of nurturing affection, and I clasped your image the closer to my heart. It is you, who, when I was most weary of existence, gifted me with a new life. You breathed into me a part of your own spirit; my soul feels that influence, and becomes more sacred. I have shut myself from the idlers who would molest me; I have built a temple in my heart; I have set within it a divinity; and the vanities of the world shall not profane the spot which has been consecrated to *you*. Our parting, Emily — do you recall it? Your hand clasped in mine; your cheek resting, though but for an instant, on my bosom; and the tears which love called forth, but which virtue purified even at their source. Never were hearts so near, yet so divided; never was there an hour so tender, yet so unaccompanied with danger. Passion, grief, madness, all sank beneath your voice, and lay hushed like a deep sea within my soul! "Tu abbia veduto il leone ammansarsi alla sola tua voce."[1]

I tore myself from you; I hurried through the wood; I stood by the lake, on whose banks I had so often wandered with you. I bared my breast to the winds; I bathed my temples with the waters. Fool that I was! the fever, the fever was within! But it is not thus, my adored and beautiful friend, that I should console and support you. Even as I write, passion melts into tenderness, and pours itself in softness over your remembrance. The virtue so gentle, yet so strong; the feelings so kind, yet so holy; the tears which wept over the decision your lips proclaimed, — these are the recollections which come over me like dew. Let your own heart, my Emily, be your reward; and know that your lover only forgets that he *adores*, to remember that he *respects* you.

FROM THE SAME TO THE SAME.

—— Park.

I could not bear the tumult and noise of London. I sighed for solitude, that I might muse over your remembrance undisturbed. I came here yesterday. It is the home of my childhood. I am surrounded on all sides by the scenes and images consecrated by the fresh recollections of my unsullied years. *They* are not changed. The seasons which come and depart renew in them the havoc which they make. If the December destroys, the April revives; but man has but one spring, and the desolation of the heart but one winter! In this very room have I sat and brooded over dreams and hopes which — But no matter, — those dreams could never show me a vision to equal *you*, or those hopes hold out to me a blessing so precious as your love.

Do you remember, or rather can you ever forget, that moment in which the great depths of our souls were revealed? Ah! not in the scene in which such vows should have been whispered to your ear, and your tenderness have blushed its reply. The passion concealed in darkness was

[1] Ultime lettere di Jacopo Ortis.

revealed in danger; and the love which in life was forbidden was our comfort amidst the terrors of death! And that long and holy kiss, the first, the only moment in which our lips shared the union of our souls! — do not tell me that it is wrong to recall it! do not tell me that I sin, when I own to you the hours I sit alone, and nurse the delirium of that voluptuous remembrance. The feelings you have excited may render me wretched, but not guilty; for the love of *you* can only *hallow* the heart, — it is a fire which consecrates the altar on which it burns. I feel, even from the hour that I loved, that my soul has become more pure. I could not believe that *I* was capable of so unearthly an affection, or that the love of woman could possess that divinity of virtue which I worship in yours. The world is no fosterer of our young visions of purity and passion; embarked in its pursuits, and acquainted with its pleasures, while the latter sated me with what is evil, the former made me incredulous to what is pure. I considered your sex as a problem which my experience had already solved. Like the French philosophers, who lose truth by endeavouring to condense it, and who forfeit the *moral* from their regard to the *maxim*, I concentrated my knowledge of women into aphorisms and antitheses; and I did not dream of the exceptions, if I did not find myself deceived in the general conclusion. I confess that I erred; I renounce from this moment the colder reflections of my manhood, — the fruits of a bitter experience, the wisdom of an inquiring yet agitated life. I return with transport to my earliest visions of beauty and love; and I dedicate them upon the altar of my soul to you, who have embodied and concentrated and breathed them into life!

EXTRACTS FROM THE JOURNAL OF LADY EMILY MANDEVILLE.

Monday. — This is the most joyless day in the whole week, for it can bring me no letter from him. I rise listlessly, and read over again and again the last letter I received from him. Useless task! it is graven on my heart! I long only for the day to be over, because to-morrow I may, perhaps, hear from him again. When I wake at night from my disturbed and broken sleep, I look if the morning is near, — not because it gives light and life, but because it may bring tidings of him. When his letter is brought to me, I keep it for minutes unopened; I feed my eyes on the handwriting; I examine the seal; I press it with my kisses, before I indulge myself in the luxury of reading it. I then place it in my bosom, and take it thence only to read it again and again, — to moisten it with my tears of gratitude and love, and, alas! of penitence and remorse! What can be the end of this affection? I dare to hope neither that it may continue nor that it may cease; in either case I am wretched forever!

Monday night, twelve o'clock. — They observe my paleness, — the tears which tremble in my eyes, the listlessness and dejection of my manner. I think Mrs. Dalton guesses the cause. Humbled and debased in my own mind, I fly, Falkland, for refuge to you! Your affection cannot raise me to my former state, but it can reconcile — no — not reconcile, but support me in my present. This dear letter, I kiss it again — oh! that to-morrow were come!

Tuesday. — Another letter, so kind, so tender, so encouraging: would that I deserved his praises! alas! I sin even in reading them. I know that I ought to struggle more against my feelings. *Once* I attempted it; I prayed to Heaven to support me; I put away from me everything that could recall him to my mind, — for three days I would not open his letters. I could then resist no longer; and my weakness became the more confirmed from the feebleness of the struggle. I remember one day that he told us of a beautiful passage in one of the ancients, in which the bitterest curse against the wicked is that they may see virtue, but not be able to obtain it,[1] — *that* punishment is mine!

Wednesday. — My boy has been with me: I see him now from the windows gathering the field-flowers, and running after every butterfly which comes across him. Formerly he made all my delight and occupation; now he is even dearer

[1] Persius.

to me than ever, but he no longer engrosses all my thoughts. I turn over the leaves of this journal: once it noted down the little occurrences of the day; it marks nothing now but the monotony of sadness. *He* is not here, — *he* cannot come. What event then *could* I notice ?

FROM ERASMUS FALKLAND, ESQ., TO LADY EMILY MANDEVILLE.[1]

—— Park.

If you knew how I long, how I thirst, for one word from you, — one word to say you are well, and have not forgotten me! — but I will not distress you. You will guess my feelings, and do justice to the restraint I impose on them, when I make no effort to alter your resolution not to write. I know that it is just, and I bow to my sentence; but can you blame me if I am restless and if I repine? It is past twelve; I always write to you at night. It is then, my own love, that my imagination can the more readily transport me to you; it is then that my spirit holds with you a more tender and undivided commune. In the day the world can force itself upon my thoughts, and its trifles usurp the place which "I love to keep for only thee and Heaven;" but in the night all things recall you the more vividly,—the stillness of the gentle skies, the blandness of the unbroken air, the stars, so holy in their loveliness, all speak and breathe to me of you. I think your hand is clasped in mine; and I again drink the low music of your voice, and imbibe again in the air the breath which has been perfumed by your lips. You seem to stand in my lonely chamber in the light and stillness of a spirit, who has wandered on earth to teach us the love which is felt in Heaven.

I cannot, believe me, — I cannot endure this separation long; it must be more or less. You must be mine forever, or our parting must be without a mitigation, which is rather a cruelty than a relief. If you will not accompany me, I will leave this country alone. I must not wean myself from your image by degrees, but break from the enchantment at once.

[1] Most of the letters from Falkland to Lady E. Mandeville I have thought it expedient to suppress.

And when, Emily, I am once more upon the world, when no tidings of my fate shall reach your ear, and all its power of alienation be left to the progress of time, — then, when you will at last have forgotten me, when your peace of mind will be restored, and, having no struggles of conscience to undergo, you will have no remorse to endure, — then, Emily, when we are indeed divided, let the scene which has witnessed our passion, the letters which have recorded my vow, the evil we have suffered, and the temptation we have overcome, let these in our old age be remembered, and in declaring to Heaven that we were innocent, add also — *that we loved.*

FROM DON ALPHONSO D'AGUILAR TO DON ——.

LONDON.

Our cause gains ground daily. The great, indeed the only ostensible, object of my mission is nearly fulfilled; but I have another charge and attraction which I am now about to explain to you. You know that my acquaintance with the English language and country arose from my sister's marriage with Mr. Falkland. After the birth of their only child I accompanied them to England; I remained with them for three years, and I still consider those days amongst the whitest in my restless and agitated career. I returned to Spain; I became engaged in the troubles and dissensions which distracted my unhappy country. Years rolled on, *how* I need not mention to *you.* One night they put a letter into my hands; it was from my sister; it was written on her deathbed. Her husband had died suddenly. She loved him as a Spanish woman loves, and she could not survive his loss. Her letter to me spoke of her country and her son. Amid the new ties she had formed in England, she had never forgotten the land of her fathers.

"I have already," she said, "taught my boy to remember that he has two countries; that the one, prosperous and free, may afford him his pleasures; that the other, struggling and debased, demands from him his duties. If, when he has attained the age in which you can judge of his character, he is respectable only from his rank, and valuable only from his wealth; if neither his head nor his heart will make him useful to *our* cause, suffer him to remain undisturbed in his prosperity *here;* but if, as I presage, he becomes worthy of the blood which he bears in his veins, then I conjure you, my brother, to remind him that he has been sworn by me on my death-bed to the most sacred of earthly altars."

Some months since, when I arrived in England, before I ventured to find him out in person, I resolved to inquire into his character. Had he been as the young and the rich generally are, — had dissipation become habitual to him, and frivolity grown around him as a second nature, — then I should have acquiesced in the former injunction of my sister much more willingly than I shall now obey the latter. I find that he is perfectly acquainted with our language, that he has placed a large sum in our Funds, and that from the general liberality of his sentiments he is as likely to espouse, as (in that case) he would be certain, from his high reputation for talent, to serve, our cause. I am, therefore, upon the eve of seeking him out. I understand that he is living in perfect retirement in the county of ——, in the immediate neighbourhood of Mr. Mandeville, an Englishman of considerable fortune, and warmly attached to our cause.

Mr. Mandeville has invited me to accompany him down to his estate for some days, and I am too anxious to see my nephew not to accept eagerly of the invitation. If I can persuade Falkland to aid us, it will be by the influence of his name, his talents, and his wealth. It is not of him that we can ask the stern and laborious devotion to which we have consecrated ourselves. The perfidy of friends, the vigilance of foes, the rashness of the bold, the cowardice of the wavering; strife in the closet, treachery in the senate, death in the field, — *these* constitute the fate we have pledged ourselves to bear. Little can any who do not endure it imagine of the life to which those who share the contests of an agitated and distracted country are doomed; but if they know not our griefs, neither can they dream of our consolation. We move like the delineation of Faith, over a barren and desert soil: the rock and the thorn and the stings of the adder are round our feet; but we clasp a crucifix to our hearts for our comfort, and we fix our eyes upon the heavens for our hope!

EXTRACTS FROM THE JOURNAL OF LADY EMILY MANDEVILLE.

Wednesday. — His letters have taken a different tone: instead of soothing, they add to my distress; but I deserve all, — all that can be inflicted upon me. I have had a letter from Mr. Mandeville. He is coming down here for a few days, and intends bringing some friends with him. He mentions particularly a Spaniard, — *the uncle of Mr. Falkland, whom he asks if I have seen.* The Spaniard is particularly anxious to meet his nephew, — he does not then know that Falkland is gone. It will be some relief to see Mr. Mandeville alone; but even then how shall I meet him? What shall I say when he observes my paleness and alteration? I feel bowed to the very dust.

Thursday evening. — Mr. Mandeville has arrived; fortunately, it was late in the evening before he came, and the darkness prevented his observing my confusion and alteration. He was kinder than usual. Oh, how bitterly my heart avenged him! He brought with him the Spaniard, Don Alphonso d'Aguilar; I think there is a faint family likeness between him and Falkland. Mr. Mandeville brought also a letter from Julia. She will be here the day after to-morrow. The letter is short, but kind: she does not allude to *him;* it is some days since I heard from him.

FROM ERASMUS FALKLAND, ESQ., TO THE HON. FREDERICK MONKTON.

I have resolved, Monkton, to go to her again! I am sure that it will be better for both of us to meet once more; perhaps, to unite forever! None who have once loved me can easily forget me. I do not say this from vanity, because I owe it not to my being *superior* to, but *different* from, others. I am sure that the remorse and affliction she feels now are far greater than she would experience, even were she more guilty, and with me. *Then,* at least, she would have some one to soothe and sympathize in whatever she might endure. To one so pure as Emily, the full crime is already incurred. It is not the innocent who insist upon that nice line of morality between the thought and the action: such distinctions require reflection, experience, deliberation, prudence of head, or coldness of heart; these are the traits, not of the guileless, but of the worldly. It is the *affections*, not the *person*, of a virtuous woman, which it is difficult to obtain: that difficulty is the safeguard to her chastity; that difficulty I have, in this instance, overcome. I have endeavoured to live without Emily, but in vain. Every moment of absence only taught me the impossibility. In twenty-four hours I shall see her again. I feel my pulse rise into fever at the very thought.

Farewell, Monkton. My next letter, I hope, will record my triumph.

BOOK III.

EXTRACTS FROM THE JOURNAL OF LADY EMILY MANDEVILLE.

Friday. — Julia is here, and so kind! She has not mentioned *his* name, but she sighed so deeply when she saw my pale and sunken countenance that I threw myself into her arms and cried like a child. We had no need of other explanation: those tears spoke at once my confession and my repentance. No letter from him for several days! Surely he is not ill! how miserable that thought makes me!

Saturday. — A note has just been brought me from him. He is come back — *here!* Good heavens! how very imprudent! I am so agitated that I can write no more.

Sunday. — I have seen him! Let me repeat that sentence, — *I have seen him.* Oh that moment! did it not atone for all that I have suffered? I dare not write everything he said, but he wished me to fly with him — *him!* what happiness, yet what guilt, in the very thought! Oh! this foolish heart — would that it might break! I feel too well the sophistry of his arguments, and yet I cannot resist them. He seems to have thrown a spell over me, which precludes even the effort to escape.

Monday. — Mr. Mandeville has asked several people in the country to dine here to-morrow, and there is to be a ball in the evening. Falkland is of course invited. We shall meet then, and *how?* I have been so little accustomed to disguise my feelings, that I quite tremble to meet him with so many witnesses around. Mr. Mandeville has been so harsh to me to-day; if Falkland ever looked at me so, or ever said one such word, my heart would indeed break. What is it Alfieri says about the two demons to whom he is forever a prey? "La mente e il cor in perpetua lite." Alas! at times I start from my reveries with such a keen sense of agony and shame! How, how am I fallen!

Tuesday. — He is to come here to-day, and I shall see him!

Wednesday morning. — The night is over, thank Heaven! Falkland came late to dinner: every one else was assembled. How gracefully he entered! how superior he seemed to all the crowd that stood around him! He appeared as if he were resolved to exert powers which he had disdained before. He entered into the conversation, not only with such brilliancy, but with such a blandness and courtesy of manner! There was no scorn on his lip, no haughtiness on his forehead, — nothing which showed him for a moment conscious of his immeasurable superiority over every one present. After dinner, as we retired, I caught his eyes. What volumes they told! — and then I had to listen to his praises, *and say nothing.* I felt angry even in my pleasure. Who but I had a right to speak of him so well?

The ball came on; I felt languid and dispirited. Falkland did not dance. He sat himself by me; he urged me to — O God! O God! would that I were dead!

FROM ERASMUS FALKLAND, ESQ., TO LADY EMILY MANDEVILLE.

How are you this morning, my adored friend? You seemed pale and ill when we parted last night, and I shall be *so* unhappy till I hear something of you. O Emily, when you listened to me with those tearful and downcast looks; when I saw your bosom heave at every word which I whispered in your ear; when, as I accidentally touched your hand, I felt it tremble beneath my own, — oh! was there nothing in those moments at your heart which pleaded for me more eloquently than words? Pure and holy as you are, you know not, it is true, the feelings which burn and madden in me. When you are beside me, your hand, if it trembles, is not on fire; your voice, if it is more subdued, does not falter with the emotions it dares not express; your heart is not, like mine, devoured by a parching and wasting flame; your sleep is not turned by restless and turbulent dreams from the healthful renewal, into the very consumer, of life. No, Emily! God forbid that you *should* feel the guilt, the agony which preys upon me; but at least, in the fond and gentle tenderness of your heart, there must be a voice you find it difficult to silence. Amidst all the fictitious ties and fascinations of art, you cannot dismiss from your bosom the unconquerable impulses of nature. What is it you fear? — you will answer, *disgrace!* But *can* you feel it, Emily, when you share it with me? Believe me that the love which is nursed through shame and sorrow is of a deeper and holier nature than that which is reared in pride, and fostered in joy. But, if not shame, it is guilt, perhaps, which you dread? Are you then so innocent *now?* The adultery of the heart is no less a crime than that of the deed; and — yet I will not deceive you — it *is* guilt to which I tempt you! — *it is* a fall from the proud eminence you hold now. I grant this, and I offer you nothing in recompense but my love. If you loved like me, you would feel that it was something of pride, of triumph, to dare all things, even crime, for the one to whom all things are as nought! As for me, I know that if a voice from Heaven told me to desert you, I would only clasp you the closer to my heart!

I tell you, my own love, that when your hand is in mine, when your head rests upon my bosom, when those soft and thrilling eyes shall be fixed upon my own, when every sigh shall be mingled with my breath, and every tear be kissed away at the very instant it rises from its source, — I tell you that then you shall only feel that every pang of the past, and every fear for the future, shall be but a new link to bind us the firmer to each other. Emily, my life, my love, you cannot, if you would, desert me. Who can separate the waters which are once united, or divide the hearts which have met and mingled into one?

Since they had once more met, it will be perceived that Falkland had adopted a new tone in expressing his passion to Emily. In the book of guilt another page, branded in a deeper and more burning character, had been turned. He lost no opportunity of summoning the earthlier emotions to the support of his cause. He wooed her fancy with the golden language of poetry, and strove to arouse the latent feelings of her sex by the soft magic of his voice, and the passionate meaning it conveyed. But at times there came over him a deep and keen sentiment of remorse; and even as his experienced and practised eye saw the moment of his triumph approach, he felt that the success he was hazarding his own soul and hers to obtain might bring him a momentary transport, but not a permanent happiness. There is always this difference in the love of women and of men: that in the former, when once admitted, it engrosses all the sources of thought, and excludes every object but itself; but in the latter, it is shared with all the former reflections and feelings which the past yet bequeaths us, and can neither (however powerful be its nature) constitute *the whole* of our happiness or woe. The love of man in his maturer years is not indeed so much a new emotion, as a revival and concentration of all his departed affections to others; and the deep and intense nature of Falkland's passion for Emily was linked with the recollections of whatever he had formerly cherished as tender or dear; it touched, it awoke a long chain of young and enthusiastic feelings, which arose, perhaps, the fresher from their slumber. Who, when he turns to recall his first and fondest associations; when he throws off, one by one, the layers of earth and stone which have grown and hardened over the records of the past, — who has not been surprised to discover how fresh and unimpaired those buried treasures rise again upon his heart? They have been laid up in the storehouse of Time; they have not perished; their very concealment has preserved them! *We remove the lava, and the world of a gone day is before us!*

The evening of the day on which Falkland had written the above letter was rude and stormy. The various streams with which the country abounded were swelled by late rains into an unwonted rapidity and breadth; and their voices blended with the rushing sound of the winds, and the distant roll of the thunder, which began at last sullenly to subside. The whole of the scene around L—— was of that savage yet sublime character which suited well with the wrath of the aroused elements. Dark woods, large tracts of unenclosed heath, abrupt variations of hill and vale, and a dim and broken outline beyond of uninterrupted mountains, formed the great features of that romantic country.

It was filled with the recollections of his youth, and of the wild delight which he took then in the convulsions and varieties of nature, that Falkland roamed abroad that evening. The dim shadows of years, crowded with concealed events and corroding reflections, all gathered around his mind, and the gloom and tempest of the night came over him like the sympathy of a friend.

He passed a group of terrified peasants; they were cowering under a tree. The oldest hid his head and shuddered; but the youngest looked steadily at the lightning which played at fitful intervals over the mountain stream that rushed rapidly by their feet. Falkland stood beside them unnoticed and silent, with folded arms and a scornful lip. To him, nature, heaven, earth, had nothing for fear, and everything for reflection. In youth, thought he (as he contrasted the fear felt at one period of life with the indifference at another), there are so many objects to divide and distract life, that we are scarcely sensible of the collected conviction that we live. We lose the sense of what *is* by thinking rather of what is *to be*. But the old, who have no future to expect, are more vividly alive to the present, and they feel death more, because they have a more settled and perfect impression of existence.

He left the group, and went on alone by the margin of the winding and swelling stream. "It is [said a certain philosopher] in the conflicts of Nature that man most feels his littleness." Like all general maxims, this is only partially true. The mind, which takes its first ideas from perception, must take also its tone from the character of the objects perceived. In mingling our spirits with the great elements, we partake of their sublimity; we awaken thought from the secret depths where it had lain concealed; our feelings are too excited to remain riveted to ourselves; they blend with the mighty powers which are abroad; and as, in the agitations of men, the individual arouses from himself to become a part of the crowd, so in the convulsions of Nature we are equally awakened from the littleness of self, to be lost in the grandeur of the conflict by which we are surrounded.

Falkland still continued to track the stream: it wound its way through Mandeville's grounds, and broadened at last into the lake which was so consecrated to his recollections. He paused at that spot for some moments, looking carelessly over the wide expanse of waters, now dark as night, and now flashing into one mighty plain of fire beneath the coruscations of the lightning. The clouds swept on in massy columns, dark and aspiring, veiling, while they rolled up to, the great heavens, like the shadows of human doubt. Oh! weak, weak was that dogma of the philosopher! There is a *pride* in the storm which, according to his doctrine, would debase us; a stirring music in its roar; even a savage joy in its destruction: for we can exult in a defiance of its power, even while we share in its triumphs, in a consciousness of a superior spirit within us to that which is around. We can mock at the fury of the elements, for they are less terrible than the passions of the heart; at the devastations of the awful skies, for they are less desolating than the wrath of man; at the convulsions of that surrounding nature which has no peril, no terror to the soul, which is more indestructible and eternal than itself. Falkland turned towards the house which contained *his* world; and as the lightning revealed at intervals the white columns of the porch, and wrapped in sheets of fire, like a spectral throng, the tall and waving trees by which it was encircled, and then as suddenly ceased, and "the jaws of darkness" devoured up the scene, he compared, with that bitter alchemy of feeling which resolves all into one crucible of thought, those alternations of sight and shadow to the history of his own guilty love, — that passion whose birth was the womb of Night; shrouded in darkness, surrounded by storms, and receiving only from the angry heavens a momentary brilliance, more terrible than its customary gloom.

As he entered the saloon, Lady Margaret advanced towards him. "My dear Falkland," said she, "how good it is in you to come in such a night. We have been watching the skies till Emily grew terrified at the lightning; *formerly* it did not alarm her." And Lady Margaret turned, utterly unconscious of the reproach she had conveyed, towards Emily.

Did not Falkland's look turn also to that spot? Lady Emily was sitting by the harp which Mrs. St. John appeared to be most seriously employed in tuning; her countenance was bent downwards, and burning beneath the blushes called forth by the gaze which she *felt* was upon her.

There was in Falkland's character a peculiar dislike to all outward display of less worldly emotions. He had none of the vanity most men have in conquest; he would not have had any human being know that he was loved. He was right! No altar should be so unseen and inviolable as the human heart! He saw at once and relieved the embarrassment he had caused. With the remarkable fascination and grace of manner so peculiarly his own, he made his excuses to Lady Margaret for his disordered dress; he charmed his uncle, Don Alphonso, with a quotation from Lopez de Vega; he inquired tenderly of Mrs. Dalton touching the health of her Italian grayhound; and then — nor till then — he ventured to approach Emily, and speak to her in that soft tone, which, like a fairy language, is understood only by the person it addresses. Mrs. St. John rose and left the harp; Falkland took her seat. He bent down to whisper Emily. His long hair touched her cheek! it was still wet with the night dew. She looked up as she felt it, and met his gaze: better had it been to have lost earth than to have drunk the soul's poison from that eye when it tempted to sin!

Mrs. St. John stood at some distance; Don Alphonso was speaking to her of his nephew, and of his hopes of ultimately gaining him to the cause of his mother's country. "See you not," said Mrs. St. John, and her colour went and came, "that while he has such attractions to detain him, your hopes are in vain?"

"What mean you?" replied the Spaniard; but his eye had followed the direction she had given it, and the question came only from his lips. Mrs. St. John drew him to a still remoter corner of the room, and it was in the conversation that then ensued between them, that they agreed to unite for the purpose of separating Emily from her lover, — "I to save my friend," said Mrs. St. John, "and you your kinsman." Thus is it with human virtue, — the fair show and the good deed without, the one eternal motive of selfishness within. During the Spaniard's visit at E——, he had seen enough of Falkland to perceive the great consequence he might, from his perfect knowledge of the Spanish language, from his singular powers, and, above all, from his command of wealth, be to the cause of that party he himself had adopted. His aim, therefore, was now no longer confined to procuring Falkland's good-will and aid at home — he hoped to secure his personal assistance in Spain; and he willingly coincided with Mrs. St. John in detaching his nephew from a tie so likely to detain him from that service to which Alphonso wished he should be pledged.

Mandeville had left E—— that morning: he suspected nothing of Emily's attachment. This, on his part, was less confidence than indifference. He was one of those persons who have no existence separate from their own: his senses all turned inwards; they reproduced selfishness. Even the House of Commons was only an object of interest, because he imagined it *a part of him, not he of it.* He said, with the insect on the wheel, "Admire *our* rapidity." But did the defects of his character remove Lady Emily's guilt? No! and this, at times, was her bitterest conviction. Whoever turns to these pages for an apology for sin will be mistaken. They contain the burning records of its sufferings, its repentance, and its doom. If there be one crime in the history of woman worse than another, it is adultery. It is, in fact, the only crime to which, in ordinary life, she is exposed. Man has a thousand temptations to sin, — woman has but one; if she cannot resist it, she has no claim upon our mercy. The heavens are just! her own guilt is her punishment! Should these pages, at this moment, meet the eyes of one who has become the centre of a circle of disgrace, — the contaminator of her house, the dishonour of her children, — no matter what the excuse for her crime, no matter what the exchange of her station — in the very arms of her lover, in the very cincture of the new ties which she has chosen, — I call upon her to answer me if the fondest moments of rapture are free from humiliation, though they have forgotten remorse; and if the passion itself of her lover has not become no less the penalty than the recompense of her guilt. But at that hour of which I now write, there was neither in Emily's heart, nor in that of her seducer, any recollection of their sin. Those hearts were too full for thought, — they had forgotten everything but each other. Their love was their creation: beyond, all was night, chaos, nothing!

Lady Margaret approached them. "You will sing to us, Emily, to-night? It is *so* long since we have heard you!" It was in vain that Emily tried, — her voice failed. She looked at Falkland, and could scarcely restrain her tears. She had not yet learned the latest art which sin teaches us, — *its concealment!* "I will supply Lady Emily's place," said Falkland. *His* voice was calm, and *his* brow serene: the world had left nothing for him to learn. "Will you play the air," he said to Mrs. St. John, "that you gave us some nights ago? I will furnish the words." Mrs. St. John's hand trembled as she obeyed.

SONG.

I.

Ah, let us love while yet we may,
  Our summer is decaying;
And woe to hearts which, in their gray
  December, go a maying.

II.

Ah, let us love, while of the fire
  Time hath not yet bereft us:
With years our warmer thoughts expire,
  Till only ice is left us!

III.

We 'll fly the bleak world's bitter air,
  A brighter home shall win us;
And if our hearts grow weary there,
  We 'll find a world within us.

IV.

They preach that passion fades each hour,
  That nought will pall like pleasure;
My bee, if Love 's so frail a flower,
  Oh, haste to hive its treasure.

V.

Wait not the hour, when all the mind
  Shall to the crowd be given;
For links, which to the *million* bind,
  Shall from the *one* be riven.

VI.

But let us love while yet we may,
  Our summer is decaying;
And woe to hearts which, in their gray
  December, go a maying.

The next day Emily rose ill and feverish. In the absence of Falkland, her mind always awoke to the full sense of the guilt she had incurred. She had been brought up in the strictest, even the most fastidious, principles; and her nature was so pure, that merely to err appeared like a change in existence, — like an entrance into some new and unknown world, from which she shrank back, in terror, to herself.

Judge, then, if she easily habituated her mind to its present degradation. She sat, that morning, pale and listless; her book lay unopened before her; her eyes were fixed upon the ground, heavy with suppressed tears. Mrs. St. John entered; no one else was in the room. She sat by her, and took her hand. Her countenance was scarcely less colourless than Emily's, but its expression was more calm and composed.

"It is not too late, Emily," she said; "you have done much that you should repent, — nothing to render repentance unavailing. Forgive me, if I speak to you on this subject. It is time: in a few days your fate will be decided. I have looked on, though hitherto I have been silent: I have witnessed that eye when it dwelt upon you; I have heard that voice when it spoke to your heart. None ever resisted their influence long; do you imagine that you are the first who have found the power? Pardon me, pardon me, I beseech you, my dearest friend, if I pain you. I have known you from your childhood, and I only wish to preserve you spotless to your old age."

Emily wept, without replying. Mrs. St. John continued to argue and expostulate. What is so wavering as passion? When, at last, Mrs. St. John ceased, and Emily shed upon her bosom the hot tears of her anguish and repentance, she imagined that her resolution was taken, and that she could almost have vowed an eternal separation from her lover; Falkland came that evening, and she loved him more madly than before.

Mrs. St. John was not in the saloon when Falkland entered. Lady Margaret was reading the well-known story of Lady T—— and the Duchess of M——, in which an agreement had been made and *kept*, that the one who died first should return once more to the survivor. As Lady Margaret spoke laughingly of the anecdote, Emily, who was watching Falkland's countenance, was struck with the dark and sudden shade which fell over it. He moved in silence towards the window where Emily was sitting. "Do you believe," she said, with a faint smile, "in the possibility of such an event?"

"I believe — though I reject — nothing!" replied Falkland, "but I would give worlds for such a proof that death does not destroy."

"Surely," said Emily, "you do not deny that evidence of our immortality which we gather from the Scriptures? — are *they* not all that a voice from the dead could be?"

Falkland was silent for a few moments: he did not seem to hear the question; his eyes dwelt upon vacancy; and when he at last spoke, it was rather in commune with himself than in answer to her.

"I have watched," said he, in a low internal tone, "over the tomb; I have called, in the agony of my heart, unto her who slept beneath; I would have *dissolved my very soul* into a spell, could it have summoned before me for one, one moment the being who had once been the spirit of my life! I have been, as it were, *entranced* with the intensity of my own adjuration; I have gazed upon the empty air, and worked upon my mind to fill it with imaginings; I have called aloud unto the winds, and tasked my soul to waken their silence to reply. All was a waste, a stillness, an infinity, — without a wanderer or a voice! The dead answered me not, when I invoked them; and in the vigils of the still night I looked from the rank grass and the mouldering stones to the Eternal Heavens, as man looks from decay to immortality! Oh! that awful magnificence of repose, that living sleep, that breathing yet unrevealing divinity, spread over those still worlds! To *them* also I poured my thoughts — *but in a whisper.* I did not dare to breathe *aloud* the unhallowed anguish of my mind to the majesty of the unsympathizing stars! In the vast order of creation — in the midst of the stupendous system of universal life, my doubt and inquiry were murmured forth — *a voice crying in the wilderness, and returning without an echo, unanswered unto myself!*"

The deep light of the summer moon shone over Falkland's countenance, which Emily gazed on, as she listened, almost tremblingly, to his words. His brow was knit and hueless, and the large drops gathered slowly over it, as if wrung from the strained yet impotent tension of the thoughts within. Emily drew nearer to him, — she laid her hand upon his own.

"Listen to me," she said; "if a herald from the grave could satisfy your doubt, *I would gladly die that I might return to you!*"

"Beware," said Falkland, with an agitated but solemn voice; "the *words now so lightly spoken may be registered on high.*"

"*Be it so!*" replied Emily firmly, and she felt what she said. *Her* love penetrated beyond the tomb, and she would have forfeited all here for their union hereafter.

"In my earliest youth," said Falkland, more calmly than he had yet spoken, "I found in the present and the past of this world enough to direct my attention to the futurity of another: if I did not credit all with the enthusiast, I had no sympathies with the scorner; I sat myself down to examine and reflect; I pored alike over the pages of the philosopher and the theologian; I was neither baffled by the subtleties nor deterred by the contradictions of either. As men first ascertained the geography of the earth by observing the signs of the heavens, I did homage to the Unknown God, and sought from that worship to inquire into the reasonings of mankind. I did not confine myself to books, — all things breathing or inanimate constituted my study. From death itself I endeavoured to extract its secret; and whole nights I have sat in the crowded asylums of the dying, watching the last spark flutter and decay. Men die away as in sleep, without effort or struggle or emotion. I have looked on their countenances a moment before death, and the serenity of repose was upon them, waxing only more deep as it approached that slumber *which is never broken:* the breath grew gentler and gentler, till the lips it came from fell from each other, and all was hushed; the light had departed from the cloud, but the cloud itself, gray, cold, altered as it seemed, was as before. *They died and made no sign.* They had left the labyrinth without bequeathing us its clew. It is in vain that I have sent my spirit into the land of shadows, — it has borne back no witnesses of its inquiry. As Newton said of himself, 'I picked up a few shells by the seashore, but the great ocean of truth lay undiscovered before me.'"

There was a long pause. Lady Margaret had sat down to chess with the Spaniard. No look was upon the lovers; their eyes met, and with that one glance the whole current of their thoughts was changed. The blood, which a moment before had left Falkland's cheek so colourless, rushed back to it again. The love which had so penetrated and pervaded his whole system, and which abstruser and colder reflection had just calmed, thrilled through his frame with redoubled power. As if by an involuntary and mutual impulse, their lips met: he threw his arm round her; he strained her to his bosom.

"Dark as my thoughts are," he whispered, "evil as has been my life, will you not yet soothe the one, and guide the other? My Emily! my love! the *Heaven to the tumultuous ocean of my heart!* will you not be mine, mine only — wholly — and forever?" She did not answer, she did not turn from his embrace. Her cheek flushed as his breath stole over it, and her bosom heaved beneath the arm which encircled that empire so devoted to him.

"Speak one word, only one word," he continued to whisper: "will you not be mine? Are you not mine at heart even at this moment?"

Her head sank upon his bosom. Those deep and eloquent eyes looked up to his through their dark lashes. "I *will* be yours," she murmured: "I am at your mercy; I have no longer any existence but in you. My only fear is, that I shall cease to be worthy of your love!"

Falkland pressed his lips once more to her own: it was his only answer, and the last seal to their compact. As they stood before the open lattice, the still and unconscious moon looked down upon that record of guilt. There was not a cloud in the heavens to dim *her* purity; the very winds of night had hushed themselves to do her homage; all was silent but *their* hearts. They stood beneath the calm and holy skies, a guilty and devoted pair, — a fearful contrast of the sin and turbulence of this unquiet earth to the passionless serenity of the eternal heaven. The same stars, that for thousands of unfathomed years had looked upon the changes of this nether world, gleamed pale and pure and steadfast upon their burning but transitory vow. In a few years what of the condemnation or the recorders of that vow would remain? From other lips, on that spot, other oaths might be plighted; new pledges of unchangeable fidelity exchanged: and year after year, in each succession of scene and time, the same stars will look from the mystery of their untracked and impenetrable home, to mock, as now, with their immutability, the variations and shadows of mankind!

FROM ERASMUS FALKLAND, ESQ., TO LADY EMILY MANDEVILLE.

At length, then, you are to be mine,— you have consented to fly with me. In three days we shall leave this country, and have no home, no world, but in each other. We will go, my Emily, to those golden lands where Nature, the only companion we will suffer, woos us, like a mother, to find our asylum in her breast; where the breezes are languid beneath the passion of the voluptuous skies; and where the purple light that invests all things with its glory is only less tender and consecrating than the spirit which we bring. Is there not, my Emily, in the external nature which reigns over creation, and that human nature centred in ourselves, some secret and undefinable intelligence and attraction? Are not the impressions of the former as spells over the passions of the latter; and in gazing upon the loveliness around us, do we not gather, as it were, and store within our hearts, an increase of the yearning and desire of love? What can we demand from earth but its solitudes,— what from heaven but its unpolluted air? All that others would ask from either, we can find in ourselves. Wealth, honour, happiness, every object of ambition or desire, exist not for us without the circle of our arms! But the bower that surrounds us shall not be unworthy of your beauty or our love. Amidst the myrtle and the vine, and the valleys where the summer sleeps, and the rivers that murmur the memories and the legends of old; amidst the hills and the glossy glades, and the silver fountains, still as beautiful as if the Nymph and Spirit yet held and decorated an earthly home,— amidst these we will make the couch of our bridals, and the moon of Italian skies shall keep watch on our repose.

Emily! Emily! — how I love to repeat and to linger over that beautiful name! If to see, to address, and, more than all, to touch you, has been a rapture, what word can I find in the vocabulary of happiness to express the realization of that hope which now burns within me,— to mingle our youth together into one stream, wheresoever it flows; to respire the same breath; to be almost blent in the same existence; to grow, as it were, on one stem, and knit into a *single* life the feelings, the wishes, the *being* of both!

To-night I shall see you again: let one day more intervene and — I cannot conclude the sentence! As I have written, the tumultuous happiness of hope has come over me to confuse and overwhelm everything else. At this moment my pulse riots with fever; the room swims before my eyes; everything is indistinct and jarring,— a chaos of emotions. Oh, that happiness should ever have such excess!

When Emily received and laid this letter to her heart, she felt nothing in common with the spirit which it breathed. With that quick transition and inconstancy of feeling common in women, and which is as frequently their safety as their peril, her mind had already repented of the weakness of the last evening, and relapsed into the irresolution and bitterness of her former remorse. Never had there been in the human breast a stronger contest between conscience and passion,— if, indeed, the extreme softness (notwithstanding its power) of Emily's attachment could be called passion: it was rather a love that had refined by the increase of its own strength; it contained nothing but the primary guilt of conceiving it, which that order of angels, *whose nature is love,* would have sought to purify away. To see him, to live with him, to count the variations of his countenance and voice, to touch his hand at moments when waking, and watch over his slumbers when he slept,— this was the essence of her wishes, and constituted the limit to her desires. Against the temptations of the present was opposed the whole history of the past. Her mind wandered from each to each, wavering and wretched, as the impulse of the moment impelled it. Hers was not, indeed, a strong character; her education and habits had weakened, while they rendered more feminine and delicate, a nature originally too soft. Every recollection of former purity called to her with the loud voice of duty, as a warning from the great guilt she was about to incur; and whenever she thought of her child,— that centre of fond and sinless sensations, where once she had so wholly garnered up her heart,— her feelings melted at once from the object which had so wildly held them riveted as by a spell, to dissolve and lose themselves in the great and sacred fountain of a mother's love.

When Falkland came that evening, she was sitting at a corner of the saloon, apparently occupied in reading; but her eyes were fixed upon her boy, whom Mrs. St. John was endeavouring at the opposite end of the room to amuse. The child, who was fond of Falkland, came up to him as he entered: Falkland stooped to kiss him; and Mrs. St. John said, in a low voice which just reached his ear, "Judas, too, kissed before he betrayed." Falkland's colour changed: he felt the sting the words were intended to convey. On that child, now so innocently caressing him, he was indeed about to inflict a disgrace and injury the most sensible and irremediable in his power. But who ever indulges reflection in passion? He banished the remorse from his mind as instantaneously as it arose; and, seating himself by Emily, endeavoured to inspire her with a portion of the joy and hope which animated himself. Mrs. St. John watched them with a jealous and anxious eye: she had already seen how useless had been her former attempt to arm Emily's conscience effectually against her lover; but she resolved at least to renew the impression she had then made. The danger was imminent, and any remedy must be prompt; and it was something to protract, even if she could not finally break off, a union against which were arrayed all the angry feelings of jealousy, as well as the better affections of the friend. Emily's eye was already brightening beneath the words that Falkland whispered in her ear, when Mrs. St. John approached her. She placed herself on a chair beside them, and unmindful of Falkland's bent and angry brow, attempted to create a general and commonplace conversation. Lady Margaret had invited two or three people in the neighbourhood; and when these came in, music and cards were resorted to immediately, with that English *politesse*, which takes the earliest opportunity to show that the conversation of our friends is the last thing for which we have invited them. But Mrs. St. John never left the lovers; and at last, when Falkland, in despair at her obstinacy, arose to join the card-table, she said, "Pray, Mr. Falkland, were you not intimate at one time with ——, who eloped with Lady ——?"

"I knew him but slightly," said Falkland; and then added, with a sneer, "the only times I ever met him were at your house."

Mrs. St. John, without noticing the sarcasm, continued. "What an unfortunate affair that proved! They were very much attached to one another in early life,—the *only* excuse, perhaps, for a woman's breaking her subsequent vows. They eloped. The remainder of their history is briefly told: it is that of all who forfeit everything for passion, and forget that of everything it is the briefest in duration. He who had sacrificed his honour for her, sacrificed her also as lightly for another. She could not bear his infidelity; and how could she reproach him? In the very act of yielding to, she had become unworthy of, his love. She *did not* reproach him,—she died of a broken heart. I saw her just before her death, for I was distantly related to her, and I could not forsake her utterly even in her sin. She then spoke to me only of the child by her former marriage, whom she had left in the years when it most needed her care: she questioned me of its health, its education, its very growth: the minutest thing was not beneath her inquiry. His tidings were all that brought back to her mind 'the redolence of joy and spring.' I brought that child to her one day: *he* at least had never forgotten her. How bitterly both wept when they were separated! and she — poor, poor Ellen, — an hour after their separation was no more!" There was a pause for a few minutes. Emily was deeply affected. Mrs. St. John had anticipated the effect she had produced, and concerted the method to increase it. "It is singular," she resumed, "that, the evening before her elopement, some verses were sent to her anonymously, — I do not think, Emily, that you have ever seen them. Shall I sing them to you now?" and, without waiting for a reply, she placed herself at the piano; and with a low but sweet voice, greatly aided in effect by the extreme feeling of her manner, she sang the following verses: —

TO ——.

I.

And wilt thou leave that happy home,
  Where once it was so sweet to live?
Ah, think, before thou seek'st to roam,
  What safer shelter Guilt can give!

II.

The Bird may rove, and still regain
  With spotless wings, her wonted rest;
But home, once lost, is ne'er again
  Restored to Woman's erring breast!

III.

If wandering o'er a world of flowers,
  The heart at times would ask repose;
But *thou* wouldst lose the only bowers
  Of rest amid a world of woes.

IV.

Recall thy youth's unsullied vow,
  The past which on thee smiled so fair;
Then turn from thence to picture now
  The frowns thy future fate must wear!

V.

No hour, no hope, can bring relief
  To her who hides a blighted name;
For hearts unbowed by stormiest *grief*
  Will break beneath one breeze of *shame!*

VI.

And when thy child's deserted years
  Amid life's early woes are thrown,
Shall menial bosoms soothe the tears
  That should be shed on thine alone?

VII.

When on thy name his lips shall call,
  (That tender name, the earliest taught!)
Thou wouldst not Shame and Sin were all
  The memories linked around its thought!

VIII.

If Sickness haunt his infant bed,
  Ah! what could then replace thy care?
Could hireling steps as gently tread
  As if a Mother's soul was there?

IX.

Enough! 't is not too late to shun
  The bitter draught thyself wouldst fill;
The latest link is not undone,
  Thy bark is in the haven still.

X.

If doomed to grief through life thou art,
  'T is thine at least unstained to die!
Oh, better break at once thy heart
  Than rend it from its holiest tie!

It were vain to attempt to describe Emily's feelings when the song ceased. The scene floated before her eyes indistinct and dark. The violence of the emotions she attempted to conceal pressed upon her almost to choking. She rose, looked at Falkland with one look of such anguish and despair that it froze his very heart, and left the room without uttering a word. A moment more, they heard a noise,—a fall. They rushed out; Emily was stretched on the ground, apparently lifeless. *She had broken a blood vessel!*

BOOK IV.

FROM MRS. ST. JOHN TO ERASMUS FALKLAND, ESQ.

At last I can give a more favourable answer to your letters. Emily is now *quite* out of danger. Since the day you forced yourself, with such a disinterested regard for her health and reputation, into her room, she grew (no thanks to your forbearance) gradually better. I trust that she will be able to see you in a few days. I hope this the more, because she now feels and decides that it will be for the last time. You have, it is true, injured her happiness for life: her virtue, thank Heaven, is yet spared; and though you have made her wretched, you will never, I trust, succeed in making her despised.

You ask me, with some menacing and more complaint, why I am so bitter against you. I will tell you. I not only know Emily, and feel confident, from that knowledge, that nothing can recompense her for the reproaches of conscience, but I know *you*, and am convinced that you are the last man to render her happy. I set aside, for the moment, all rules of religion and morality in general, and speak to you (to use the cant and abused phrase) "without prejudice" as to the particular instance. Emily's nature is soft and susceptible, yours fickle and wayward in the extreme. The smallest change or caprice in you, which would not be noticed by a mind less delicate, would wound *her* to the heart. You know that the very softness of her character arises from its want of strength. Consider, for a moment, if she could bear the humiliation and disgrace which visit so heavily the offences of an English wife. She has been brought up in the strictest notions of morality; and, in a mind not naturally strong, nothing can efface the first impressions of education. She is not — indeed she is not — fit for a life of sorrow or degradation. In another character, another line of conduct might be desirable; but with regard to *her*, pause, Falkland, I beseech you, before you attempt again to destroy her forever. I have said all. Farewell.

Your, and above all, Emily's friend.

FROM ERASMUS FALKLAND, ESQ., TO LADY EMILY MANDEVILLE.

You will see me, Emily, now that you are recovered sufficiently to do so without danger. I do not ask this as a favour. If my love has deserved anything from yours, if past recollections give me any claim over you, if my nature has not forfeited the spell which it formerly possessed upon your own, I demand it as a right.

The bearer waits for your answer.

FROM LADY EMILY MANDEVILLE TO ERASMUS FALKLAND, ESQ.

See you, Falkland! Can you doubt it? Can you think for a moment that your commands can ever cease to become a law to me? Come here whenever you please. If, during my illness, they have prevented it, it was without my knowledge. I await you; but I own that this interview will be the last, if I can claim anything from your mercy.

FROM ERASMUS FALKLAND, ESQ., TO LADY EMILY MANDEVILLE.

I have seen you, Emily, and for the last time! My eyes are dry, — my hand does not tremble. I live, move, breathe, as before — and yet I have seen you for the last time! You told me — even while you leaned on my bosom, even while your lip pressed mine, — you told me (and I saw your sincerity) to spare you, and to see you no more. You told me you had no longer any will, any fate of your own; that you would, if I still continued to desire it, leave friends, home, honour, for me; but you did not disguise from me that you would in so doing leave happiness also. You did not conceal from me that I was not sufficient to constitute all your world; you threw yourself, as you had done once before, upon what you called my generosity; you did not deceive yourself then,—you have not deceived yourself now. In two weeks I shall leave England, probably forever. I have another country still more dear to me, from its afflictions and humiliation. Public ties differ but little in their nature from private; and this confession of preference of what is debased to what is exalted will be an answer to Mrs. St. John's assertion that we cannot love in disgrace as we can in honour. Enough of this. In the choice, my poor Emily, that you have made, I cannot reproach you. You have done wisely, rightly, virtuously. You said that this separation must rest rather with me than with yourself; that you would be mine the moment I demanded it. I will not now or ever accept this promise. No one, much less one whom I love so intensely, so truly as I do you, shall ever receive disgrace at my hands, unless she can feel that that disgrace would be dearer to her than glory elsewhere; that the simple fate of being mine was not so much a recompense as a reward; and that, in spite of worldly depreciation and shame, it would constitute and concentrate all her visions of happiness and pride. I am now going to bid you farewell. May you — I say this disinterestedly, and from my very heart — may you soon forget how much you have loved and yet love me! For this purpose, you cannot have a better companion than Mrs. St. John. Her opinion of me is loudly expressed, and probably true; at all events, you will do wisely to believe it. You will hear me attacked and reproached by many. I do not deny the charges; you know best what I have deserved from *you*. God bless you, Emily. Wherever I go, I shall never cease to love you as I do now. May you be happy in your child and in your conscience! Once more, God bless you, and farewell!

FROM LADY EMILY MANDEVILLE TO ERASMUS FALKLAND, ESQ.

O Falkland! you have conquered! I am yours — *yours only — wholly and forever.* When your letter came, my hand trembled so, that I could not open it for several minutes; and when I did, I felt as if the very earth had passed from my feet. You were going from your country; you were about to be lost to me forever. I could restrain myself no longer; all my virtue, my pride, forsook me at once. Yes, yes, you are indeed my world! I will fly with you anywhere — everywhere. Nothing can be dreadful but not seeing you; I would be a servant, a slave, a dog, as long as I could be with you,— hear one tone of your voice, catch one glance of your eye. I scarcely see the paper before me, my thoughts are so straggling and confused. Write to me one word, Falkland; one word, and I will lay it to my heart, and be happy.

FROM ERASMUS FALKLAND TO LADY EMILY MANDEVILLE.

—— HOTEL, LONDON.

I hasten to you, Emily, my own and only love. Your letter has restored me to life. To-morrow we shall meet.

It was with mingled feelings, alloyed and embittered, in spite of the burning hope which predominated over all, that Falkland returned to E——. He knew that he was near the completion of his most ardent wishes; that he was within the grasp of a prize which included all the thousand objects of ambition, into which, among other men, the desires are divided; the only dreams he had ventured to form for years were about to kindle into life. He had every reason to be happy; — such is the inconsistency of human nature, that he was almost wretched. The morbid melancholy habitual to him threw its colourings over every emotion and idea. He knew the character of the woman whose affections he had seduced, and he trembled to think of the doom to which he was about to condemn her. With this, there came over his mind a long train of dark and remorseful recollections. Emily was not the only one whose destruction he had prepared. All who had loved him he had repaid with ruin; and *one*, the first, the fairest, and the most loved, with death.

That last remembrance more bitterly than all possessed him. It will be recollected that Falkland, in the letters which begin this work, speaking of the ties he had formed after the loss of his first love, says that it was the senses, not the affections, that were engaged. Never, indeed, since her death, till he met Emily, had his *heart* been unfaithful to her memory. Alas! none but those who have cherished in their souls an image of the death; who have watched over it for long and bitter years in secrecy and gloom; who have felt that it was to them as a holy and fairy spot which no eye but theirs could profane; who have filled all things with *recollections* as with a spell, and made the universe one wide mausoleum of the lost,— none but those can understand the mysteries of that regret which is shed over every after passion, though it be more burning and intense; that sense of sacrilege with which we fill up the haunted recesses of the spirit with a new and a living idol, and perpetrate the last act of infidelity to that buried love, which the heavens that now receive her, the earth where we beheld her, tell us, with the unnumbered voices of Nature, to worship with the incense of our faith.

His carriage stopped at the lodge. The woman who opened the gates gave him the following note: —

Mr. Mandeville is returned; I almost fear that he suspects our attachment. Julia says that if you come again to E——, she will inform him. I dare not, dearest Falkland, see you here. What is to be done? I am very ill and feverish; my brain burns so, that I can think, feel, remember nothing, but the one thought, feeling, and remembrance, — that through shame, and despite of guilt, in life and till death, I am

Yours, E. M.

As Falkland read this note, his extreme and engrossing love for Emily doubled with each word: an instant before, and the certainty of seeing her had suffered his mind to be divided into a thousand objects; now doubt united them once more into one.

He altered his route to L——, and despatched from thence a short note to Emily, imploring her to meet him that evening by the lake in order to arrange their ultimate flight. Her answer was brief and blotted with her tears; but it was assent.

During the whole of that day, at least from the moment she received Falkland's letter, Emily was scarcely sensible of a single idea; she sat still and motionless, gazing on vacancy, and seeing nothing within her mind or in the objects which surrounded her but one dreary blank. Sense, thought, feeling, even remorse, were congealed and frozen; and the tides of emotion were still, *but they were ice!*

As Falkland's servant had waited without to deliver the note to Emily, Mrs. St. John had observed him; her alarm and surprise only served to quicken her presence of mind. She intercepted Emily's answer under pretence of giving it herself to Falkland's servant. She read it, and her resolution was formed. After carefully resealing and delivering it to the servant, she went at once to Mr. Mandeville, and revealed Lady Emily's attachment to Falkland. In this act of treachery, she was solely instigated by her passions; and when Mandeville, roused from his wonted apathy to a paroxysm of indignation, thanked her again and again for the generosity of friendship which he imagined was all that actuated her communication, he dreamed not of the fierce and ungovernable jealousy which envied the very disgrace which her confession was intended to award. Well said the French enthusiast, "that the heart, the most serene to appearance, resembles that calm and glassy fountain which cherishes the monster of the Nile in the bosom of its waters." Whatever reward Mrs. St. John proposed to herself in this action, verily she has had the recompense that was her due. Those consequences of her treachery, which I hasten to relate, have ceased to others,— to *her* they remain. Amidst the pleasures of dissipation, one reflection has rankled at her mind; one dark cloud has rested between the sunshine and her soul; like the murderer in Shakspeare, the revel where she fled for forgetfulness has teemed to her with the spectres of remembrance. O thou untameable conscience! thou that never flatterest, thou that watchest over the human heart never to slumber or to sleep,— it is thou that takest from us the present, barrest to us the future, and knittest the eternal chain that binds us to the rock and the vulture of the past!

The evening came on still and dark; a breathless and heavy apprehension seemed gathered over the air; the full large clouds lay without motion in the dull sky, from between which, at long and scattered intervals, the wan stars looked out; a double shadow seemed to invest the grouped and gloomy trees that stood unwaving in the melancholy horizon. The waters of the lake lay heavy and unagitated, as the sleep of death; and the broken reflections of the abrupt and winding banks rested upon their bosoms, like the dream-like remembrance of a former existence.

The hour of the appointment was arrived: Falkland stood by the spot, gazing upon the lake before him; his cheek was flushed, his hand was parched and dry with the consuming fire within him; his pulse beat thick and rapidly; the demon of evil passions was upon his soul. He stood so lost in his own reflections, that he did not for some moments perceive the fond and tearful eye which was fixed upon him. On that brow and lip, thought seemed always so beautiful, so divine, that to disturb its repose was like a profanation of something holy; and though Emily came towards him with a light and hurried step, she paused involuntarily to gaze upon that noble countenance which realized her earliest visions of the beauty and majesty of love. He turned slowly, and perceived her; he came to her with his own peculiar smile; he drew her to his bosom in silence; he pressed his lips to her forehead: she leaned upon his bosom, and forgot all but him. Oh, if there be one feeling which makes Love, even guilty Love, a god, it is the knowledge that in the midst of this breathing world he reigns aloof and alone; and that those who are occupied with his worship know nothing of the pettiness, the strife, the bustle, which pollute and agitate the ordinary inhabitants of earth! What was now to them, as they stood alone in the deep stillness of Nature, everything that had engrossed them before they had met and loved? Even in her the recollections of guilt and grief subsided; she was only sensible of one thought,— the presence of the being who stood beside her,—

> "That ocean to the rivers of her soul."

They sat down beneath an oak; Falkland stooped to kiss the cold and pale cheek that still rested upon his breast. His kisses were like lava: the turbulent and stormy elements of sin and desire were aroused even to madness within him. He clasped her still nearer to his bosom: her lips answered to his own; they caught perhaps something of the spirit which they received; her eyes were half-closed; the bosom heaved wildly that was pressed to his beating and burning heart. The skies grew darker and darker, as the night stole over them; one low roll of thunder broke upon the curtained and heavy air,— *they* did not hear it; and yet it was the knell of peace, virtue, hope, lost, lost forever to their souls!

. . . .

They separated as they had never done before. In Emily's bosom there was a dreary void, a vast blank, over which there went a low deep voice like a Spirit's,— a sound indistinct and strange, that spoke a language she knew not; but felt that it told of woe, guilt, doom. Her senses were stunned; the vitality of her feelings was numbed and torpid,— the first herald of despair is insensibility. "To-morrow, then," said Falkland,— and his voice for the first time seemed strange and harsh to her,— "we will fly hence forever. Meet me at daybreak; the carriage shall be in attendance; we cannot now unite too soon. Would that at this very moment we were prepared!"

"To-morrow!" repeated Emily, "at daybreak!" and as she clung to him, he felt her shudder; "to-morrow — ay — to-morrow!" One kiss, one embrace, one word,— *farewell,*— and they parted.

Falkland returned to L——. A gloomy foreboding rested upon his mind, — that dim and indescribable fear, which no earthly or human cause can explain, that shrinking within self, that vague terror of the future, that grappling as it were with some unknown shade, that wandering of the spirit — whither? — that cold, cold creeping dread — of what? As he entered the house, he met his confidential servant. He gave him orders respecting the flight of the morrow, and then retired into the chamber where he slept. It was an antique and large room: the wainscot was of oak; and one broad and high window looked over the expanse of country which stretched beneath. He sat himself by the casement in silence, — he opened it; the dull air came over his forehead, not with a sense of freshness, but, like the parching atmosphere of the east, charged with a weight and fever that sank heavy into his soul. He turned; he threw himself upon the bed, and placed his hands over his face. His thoughts were scattered into a thousand indistinct forms, but over all, there was one rapturous remembrance; and that was, that the morrow was to unite him forever to her whose possession had only rendered her more dear. Meanwhile, the hours rolled on; and as he lay thus silent and still, the clock of the distant church struck with a distinct and solemn sound upon his ear. It was the half-hour after midnight. At that moment an icy thrill ran, slow and curdling, through his veins. His heart, as if with a presentiment of what was to follow, beat violently, and then stopped; life itself seemed ebbing away; cold drops stood upon his forehead; his eyelids trembled, and the balls reeled and glazed, like those of a dying man; a deadly fear gathered over him, so that his flesh quivered, and every hair in his head seemed instinct with a separate life; the very marrow of his bones crept, and his blood waxed thick and thick, as if stagnating into an ebbless and frozen substance. He started in a wild and unutterable terror. There stood, at the far end of the room, a dim and thin shape like moonlight, without outline or form; still, and indistinct, and shadowy. He gazed on, speechless and motionless; his faculties and senses seemed locked in an unnatural trance.

By degrees the shape became clearer and clearer to his fixed and dilating eye. He saw, as through a floating and mist-like veil, the features of Emily; but how changed! — sunken and hueless, and set in death. The dropping lip, from which there seemed to trickle a deep red stain like blood; the lead-like and lifeless eye; the calm, awful, mysterious repose which broods over the aspect of the dead,— all grew, as it were, from the hazy cloud that encircled them for one, one brief, agonizing moment, and then as suddenly faded away. The spell passed from his senses. He sprang from the bed with a loud cry. All was quiet. There was not a trace of what he had witnessed. The feeble light of the skies rested upon the spot where the apparition had stood; upon that spot he stood also. He stamped upon the floor — it was firm beneath his footing. He passed his hands over his body — he was awake, he was unchanged: earth, air, heaven, were around him as before. What had thus gone over his soul to awe and overcome it to such weakness? To these questions his reason could return no answer. Bold by nature, and sceptical by philosophy, his mind gradually recovered its original tone. He did not give way to conjecture; he endeavoured to discard it; he sought by natural causes to account for the apparition he had seen or imagined; and as he felt the blood again circulating in its accustomed courses, and the night air coming chill over his feverish frame, he smiled with a stern and scornful bitterness at the terror which had so shaken, and the fancy which had so deluded, his mind.

Are there not "more things in heaven and earth than are dreamed of in our philosophy"? A Spirit may hover in the air that we breathe; the depth of our most secret solitudes may be peopled by the invisible; our uprisings and our down-sittings may be marked by a witness from the grave. In our walks the dead may be behind us; in our banquets they may sit at the board; and the chill breath of the night wind that stirs the curtains of our bed may bear a message our senses receive not, from lips that once have pressed kisses on our own! Why is it that at moments there creeps over us an awe, a terror, overpowering, but undefined? Why is it that we shudder without a cause, and feel the warm life-blood stand still in its courses? *Are the dead too near?* Do unearthly wings touch us as they flit around? Has our soul any intercourse which the body shares not, though it feels, with the supernatural world, mysterious revealings, unimaginable communion, a language of dread and power, shaking to its centre the fleshly barrier that divides the spirit from its race?

How fearful is the very life which we hold! We have our being beneath a cloud, and are a marvel even to ourselves. There is not a single thought which has its affixed limits. Like circles in the water, our researches weaken as they extend, and vanish at last into the immeasurable and unfathomable space of the vast unknown. We are like children in the dark; we tremble in a shadowy and terrible void, peopled with our fancies! Life is our real night, and the first gleam of the morning, which brings us certainty, *is death.*

Falkland sat the remainder of that night by the window, watching the clouds become gray as the dawn rose, and its earliest breeze awoke. He heard the trampling of the horses beneath; he drew his cloak round him, and descended. It was on a turning of the road beyond the lodge that he directed the carriage to wait, and he then proceeded to the place appointed. Emily was not yet there. He walked to and fro with an agitated and hurried step. The impression of the night had in a great measure been effaced from his mind, and he gave himself up without reserve to the warm and sanguine hopes which he had so much reason to conceive. He thought too, at moments, of those bright climates beneath which he designed their asylum, where the very air is music, and the light is like the colourings of love; and he associated the sighs of a mutual rapture with the fragrance of myrtles, and the breath of a Tuscan heaven. Time glided on. The hour was long past, yet Emily came not! The sun rose, and Falkland turned in dark and angry discontent from its beams. With every moment his impatience increased, and at last he could restrain himself no longer. He proceeded towards the house. He stood for some time at a distance; but as all seemed still hushed in repose, he drew nearer and nearer till he reached the door: to his astonishment it was open. He saw forms passing rapidly through the hall. He heard a confused and indistinct murmur. At length he caught a glimpse of Mrs. St. John. He could command himself no more. He sprang forward, entered the door, the hall,— and caught her by a part of her dress. He could not speak, but his countenance said all which his lips refused. Mrs. St. John burst into tears when she saw him. "Good God!" she said, "why are you here? Is it possible you have yet learned—" Her voice failed her. Falkland had by this time recovered himself. He turned to the servants, who gathered around him. "Speak," he said calmly. "What has occurred?"

"My lady — my lady!" burst at once from several tongues.

"What of her?" said Falkland, with a blanched cheek, but unchanging voice.

There was a pause. At that instant a man, whom Falkland recognized as the physician of the neighbourhood, passed at the opposite end of the hall. A light, a scorching and intolerable light, broke upon him. "She is dying,— she is dead, perhaps," he said, in a low sepulchral tone, turning his eye around till it had rested upon every one present. *Not one answered.* He paused a moment, as if stunned by a sudden shock, and then sprang up the stairs. He passed the boudoir, and entered the room where Emily slept. The shutters were only partially closed: a faint light broke through, and rested on the bed; beside it bent two women. Them he neither heeded nor saw. He drew aside the curtains. He beheld— the same as he had seen it in his vision of the night before — the changed and lifeless countenance of Emily Mandeville! That face, still so tenderly beautiful, was partially turned towards him. Some dark stains upon the lip and neck told how she had died,— the blood-vessel she had broken before had burst again. The bland and soft eyes, which for him never had but *one* expression, were closed; and the long and dishevelled tresses half hid, while they contrasted, that bosom, which had but the night before first learned to thrill beneath his own. Happier in her fate than she deserved, she passed from this bitter life ere the punishment of her guilt had begun. She was not doomed to wither beneath the blight of shame nor the coldness of estranged affection. From him whom she had so worshipped, she was not condemned to bear wrong nor change. She died while his passion was yet in its spring,— before a blossom, a leaf, had faded; and she sank to repose while his kiss was yet warm upon her lip, and her last breath almost mingled with his sigh. For the woman who has erred, life has no exchange for such a death. Falkland stood mute and motionless; not one word of grief or horror escaped his lips. At length he bent down. He took the hand which lay outside the bed; he pressed it; it replied not to the pressure, but fell cold and heavy from his own. He put his cheek to her lips; not the faintest breath came from them; and then for the first time a change passed over his countenance: he pressed upon those lips one long and last kiss, and without word, or sign, or tear he turned from the chamber. Two hours afterwards he was found senseless upon the ground; it was upon the spot where he had met Emily the night before.

For weeks he knew nothing of this earth,— he was encompassed with the spectres of a terrible dream. All was confusion, darkness, horror,— a series and a change of torture! At one time he was hurried through the heavens in the womb of a fiery star, girt above and below and around with unextinguishable but unconsuming flames. Wherever he trod, as he wandered through his vast and blazing prison, the molten fire was his footing, and the breath of fire was his air. Flowers and trees and hills were in that world as in ours, but wrought from one lurid and intolerable light; and, scattered around, rose gigantic palaces and domes of the living flame, like the mansions of the city of Hell. With every moment there passed to and fro shadowy forms, on whose countenances was engraven unutterable anguish; but not a shriek, not a groan, rung through the red air; *for the doomed, who fed and inhabited the flames, were forbidden the consolation of voice.* Above there sat, fixed and black, a solid and impenetrable cloud,— *Night frozen into substance;* and from the midst there hung a banner of a pale and sickly flame, on which was written "Forever." A river rushed rapidly beside him. He stooped to slake the agony of his thirst,—the waves *were waves of fire;* and, as he started from the burning draught, he longed to shriek aloud, *and could not.* Then he cast his despairing eyes above for mercy; and saw on the livid and motionless banner "Forever."

" A change came o'er the spirit of his dream, —"

he was suddenly borne up on the winds and storms to the oceans of an eternal winter. He fell stunned and unstruggling upon the ebbless and sluggish waves. Slowly and heavily they rose over him as he sank; then came the lengthened and suffocating torture of that drowning death,—the impotent and convulsive contest with the closing waters, the gurgle, the choking, the bursting of the pent breath, the flutter of the heart, its agony, *and its stillness.* He recovered. He was a thousand fathoms beneath the sea, chained to a rock round which the heavy waters rose as a wall. He felt his own flesh rot and decay, perishing from his limbs piece by piece; and he saw the coral banks, which it requires a thousand ages to form, rise slowly from their slimy bed, and spread atom by atom, till they became a shelter for the leviathan: *their growth was his only record of eternity;* and ever and ever, around and above him, came vast and misshapen things,—the wonders of the secret deeps; and the sea serpent, the huge chimæra of the North, made its resting-place by his side, glaring upon him with a livid and death-like eye, wan, yet burning *as an expiring sun.* But over all, in every change, in every moment of that immortality, there was present one pale and motionless countenance, never turning from his own. The fiends of hell, the monsters of the hidden ocean, had no horror so awful *as the human face of the dead whom he had loved.*

The word of his sentence was gone forth. Alike through that delirium and its more fearful awakening, through the past, through the future, through the vigils of the joyless day and the broken dreams of the night, there was a charm upon his soul, a hell within himself; and the curse of his sentence was — *never to forget!*

When Lady Emily returned home on that guilty and eventful night, she stole at once to her room; she dismissed her servant, and threw herself upon the ground in that deep despair which on this earth can never again know hope. She lay there without the power to weep, or the courage to pray — how long, she knew not. Like the period before creation, her mind was a chaos of jarring elements, and knew neither the method of reflection nor the division of time.

As she rose, she heard a slight knock at the door, and her husband entered. Her heart misgave her; and when she saw him close the door carefully before he approached her, she felt as if she could have sunk into the earth, alike from her internal shame and her fear of its detection.

Mr. Mandeville was a weak, commonplace character,— indifferent in ordinary matters, but, like most imbecile minds, violent and furious when aroused. "Is this, Madam, addressed to you?" he cried, in a voice of thunder, as he placed a letter before her (it was one of Falkland's); "and this, and this, Madam?" said he, in a still louder tone, as he flung them out one after another from her own escritoire, which he had broken open.

Emily sank back, and gasped for breath. Mandeville rose, and, laughing fiercely, seized her by the arm. He grasped it with all his force. She uttered a faint scream of terror; he did not heed it. He flung her from him, and, as she fell upon the ground, the blood gushed in torrents from her lips. In the sudden change of feeling which alarm created, he raised her in his arms. *She was a corpse!* At that instant the clock struck upon his ear with a startling and solemn sound: *it was the half-hour after midnight!*

The grave is now closed upon that soft and erring heart, with its guiltiest secret unrevealed. She went to that last home with a blest and unblighted name; for her guilt was unknown, and her virtues are yet recorded in the memories of the Poor.

. . . .

They laid her in the stately vaults of her ancient line, and her bier was honoured with tears from hearts not less stricken, because their sorrow, if violent, was brief. For the dead there are many mourners, but only one monument,— the bosom which loved them *best.* The spot where the hearse rested, the green turf beneath, the surrounding trees, the gray tower of the village church, and the proud halls rising beyond,—all had witnessed the childhood, the youth, the bridal-day of the being whose last rites and solemnities they were to witness now. The very bell which rang for her birth had rung also for the marriage peal; it *now* tolled for her death. But a little while, and she had gone forth from that home of her young and unclouded years, amidst the acclamations and blessings of all, a bride, with the insignia of bridal pomp,—in the first bloom of her girlish beauty, in the first innocence of her unawakened heart,—weeping, not for the future she was entering, but for the past she was about to leave, and smiling through her tears, as if innocence had no business with grief. On the same spot where he had then waved his farewell, stood the father now. On the grass which they had then covered, flocked the peasants whose wants her childhood had relieved; by the same priest who had blessed her bridals, bent the bridegroom who had plighted its vow. There was not a tree, not a blade of grass withered. The day itself was bright and glorious; such was it when it smiled upon her nuptials. And *she*—*she*—but four little years, and all youth's innocence darkened, and earth's beauty come to dust! Alas! not for her, but the mourner whom she left! In death even love is forgotten; but in life there is no bitterness so utter as to feel everything is unchanged, except the One Being who was the soul of all,—to know *the world* is the same, but that *its sunshine* is departed.

. . . .

The noon was still and sultry. Along the narrow street of the small village of Lodar poured the wearied but yet unconquered band, which embodied in that district of Spain the last hope and energy of freedom. The countenances of the soldiers were haggard and dejected; they displayed even less of the vanity than their accoutrements exhibited of the pomp and circumstances of war. Yet their garments were such as even the peasants had disdained: covered with blood and dust, and tattered into a thousand rags, they betokened nothing of chivalry but its endurance of hardship; even the rent and sullied banners drooped sullenly along their staves, as if the winds themselves had become the minions of fortune, and disdained to swell the insignia of those whom she had deserted. The glorious music of battle was still. An air of dispirited and defeated enterprise hung over the whole array.

"Thank Heaven," said the chief, who closed the last file as it marched on to its scanty refreshment and brief repose, — "thank Heaven, we are at least out of the reach of pursuit; and the mountains, those last retreats of liberty, are before us!"

"True, Don Rafael," replied the youngest of two officers who rode by the side of the commander; "and if we can cut our passage to Mina, we may yet plant the standard of the Constitution in Madrid."

"Ay," added the elder officer, "and sing Riego's hymn in the place of the Escurial!"

"Our sons may!" said the chief, who was indeed Riego himself, "but for us all hope is over! Were we united, we could scarcely make head against the armies of France; and divided as we are, the wonder is that we have escaped so long. Hemmed in by invasion, our great enemy has been ourselves. Such has been the hostility faction has created between Spaniard and Spaniard, that we seem to have none left to waste upon Frenchmen. We cannot establish freedom if men are willing to be slaves. We have no hope, Don Alphonso, — no hope — but that of death!"

As Riego concluded this desponding answer, so contrary to his general enthusiasm, the younger officer rode on among the soldiers, cheering them with words of congratulation and comfort; ordering their several divisions; cautioning them to be prepared at a moment's notice; and impressing on their remembrance those small but essential points of discipline, which a Spanish troop might well be supposed to disregard.

When Riego and his companion entered the small and miserable hovel which constituted the head-quarters of the place, this man still remained without; and it was not till he had slackened the girths of his Andalusian horse, and placed before it the undainty provender which the *écurie* afforded, that he thought of rebinding more firmly the bandages wound around a deep and painful sabre-cut in the left arm, which for several hours had been wholly neglected. The officer whom Riego had addressed by the name of Alphonso came out of the hut just as his comrade was vainly endeavouring, with his teeth and one hand, to replace the ligature. As he assisted him, he said, "You know not, my dear Falkland, how bitterly I reproach myself for having ever persuaded you to a cause where contest seems to have no hope, and danger no glory."

Falkland smiled bitterly. "Do not deceive yourself, my dear uncle," said he; "your persuasions would have been unavailing but for the suggestions of my own wishes. I am not one of those enthusiasts who entered on your cause with high hopes and chivalrous designs: I asked but forgetfulness and excitement,—I have found them! I would not exchange a single pain I have endured for what would have constituted the pleasures of other men. But enough of this. What time, think you, have we for repose?"

"Till the evening," answered Alphonso; "our route will then most probably be directed to the Sierra Morena. The general is extremely weak and exhausted, and needs a longer rest than we shall gain. It is singular that with such weak health he should endure so great an excess of hardship and fatigue."

During this conversation they entered the hut. Riego was already asleep. As they seated themselves to the wretched provision of the place, a distant and indistinct noise was heard. It came first on their ears like the birth of the mountain wind,—low and hoarse and deep; gradually it grew loud and louder, and mingled with other sounds which they defined too well,—the hum, the murmur, the trampling of steeds, the ringing echoes of the rapid march of armed men!

They heard and knew the foe was upon them! — a moment more, and the drum beat to arms.

"By Saint Pelagio," cried Riego, who had sprung from his light sleep at the first sound of the approaching danger, unwilling to believe his fears, "it cannot be! the French are far behind;" and then, as the drum beat, his voice suddenly changed: "The enemy! the enemy! D'Aguilar, to horse!" and with those words he rushed out of the hut. The soldiers, who had scarcely begun to disperse, were soon re-collected.

In the mean while the French commander, D'Argout, taking advantage of the surprise he had occasioned, poured on his troops, which consisted solely of cavalry, undaunted and undelayed by the fire of the posts. On, on they drove like a swift cloud charged with thunder, and gathering wrath as it hurried by, before it burst in tempest on the beholders. They did not pause till they reached the farther extremity of the village; there the Spanish infantry were already formed into two squares. "Halt!" cried the French commander; the troop suddenly stopped, confronting the nearer square. There was one brief pause, — the moment before the storm. "Charge!" said D'Argout, and the word rang throughout the line up to the clear and placid sky. Up flashed the steel like lightning; on went the troop like the dash of a thousand waves when the sun is upon them; and before the breath of the riders was thrice drawn, came the crash, the shock, the slaughter of battle. The Spaniards made but a faint resistance to the impetuosity of the onset: they broke on every side beneath the force of the charge, like the weak barriers of a rapid and swollen stream; and the French troops, after a brief but bloody victory (joined by a second squadron from the rear), advanced immediately upon the Spanish cavalry. Falkland was by the side of Riego. As the troop advanced, it would have been curious to notice the contrast of expression in the face of each; the Spaniard's features lighted up with the daring enthusiasm of his nature; every trace of their usual languor and exhaustion vanished beneath the unconquerable soul that blazed out the brighter for the debility of the frame; the brow knit, the eye flashing, the lip quivering:

and close beside, the calm, stern, passionless repose that brooded over the severe yet noble beauty of Falkland's countenance. To him danger brought scorn, not enthusiasm; he rather despised than defied it. "The dastards! they waver!" said Riego, in an accent of despair, as his troop faltered beneath the charge of the French; and so saying, he spurred his steed on to the foremost line. The contest was longer, but not less decisive, than the one just concluded. The Spaniards, thrown into confusion by the first shock, never recovered themselves. Falkland, who, in his anxiety to rally and inspirit the soldiers, had advanced with two other officers beyond the ranks, was soon surrounded by a detachment of dragoons; the wound in his left arm scarcely suffered him to guide his horse; he was in the most imminent danger. At that moment D'Aguilar, at the head of his own immediate followers, cut his way into the circle, and covered Falkland's retreat; another detachment of the enemy came up, and they were a second time surrounded. In the mean while, the main body of the Spanish cavalry were flying in all directions, and Riego's deep voice was heard at intervals, through the columns of smoke and dust, calling and exhorting them in vain. D'Aguilar and his scanty troop, after a desperate skirmish, broke again through the enemy's line drawn up against their retreat. The rank closed after them, like waters when the object that pierced them has sunk. Falkland and his two companions were again environed: he saw his comrades cut to the earth before him. He pulled up his horse for one moment, clove down with one desperate blow the dragoon with whom he was engaged, and then setting his spurs to the very rowels into his horse, dashed at once through the circle of his foes. His remarkable presence of mind, and the strength and sagacity of his horse, befriended him. Three sabres flashed before him, and glanced harmless from his raised sword, like lightning on the water. The circle was passed! As he galloped towards Riego, his horse started from a dead body that lay across his path. He reined up for one instant, for the countenance, which looked upwards, struck him as familiar. What was his horror, when in that livid and distorted face he recognized his uncle! The thin grizzled hairs were besprent with gore and brains, and the blood yet oozed from the spot where the ball had passed through his temple. Falkland had but a brief interval for grief; the pursuers were close behind: he heard the snort of the foremost horse before he again put spurs into his own. Riego was holding a hasty consultation with his principal officers. As Falkland rode breathless up to them, they had decided on the conduct expedient to adopt. They led the remaining square of infantry towards the chain of mountains against which the village, as it were, leaned; and there the men dispersed in all directions. "For us," said Riego to the followers on horseback who gathered around him,—"for us the mountains still promise a shelter. We must ride, gentlemen, for our lives — Spain will want *them* yet."

Wearied and exhausted as they were, that small and devoted troop fled on into the recesses of the mountains for the remainder of that day,— twenty men out of the two thousand who had halted at Lodar. As the evening stole over them, they entered into a narrow defile; the tall hills rose on every side, covered with the glory of the setting sun, as if Nature rejoiced to grant her bulwarks as a protection to liberty. A small clear stream ran through the valley, sparkling with the last smile of the departing day; and ever and anon, from the scattered shrubs and the fragrant herbage, came the vesper music of the birds, and the hum of the wild bee.

Parched with thirst and drooping with fatigue, the wanderers sprung forward with one simultaneous cry of joy to the glassy and refreshing wave which burst so unexpectedly upon them; and it was resolved that they should remain for some hours in a spot where all things invited them to the repose they so imperiously required. They flung themselves at once upon the grass; and such was their exhaustion, that rest was almost synonymous with sleep. Falkland alone could not immediately forget himself in repose; the face of his uncle, ghastly and disfigured, glared upon his eyes whenever he closed them. Just, however, as he was sinking into an unquiet and fitful doze, he heard steps approaching; he started up, and perceived two men, one a peasant, the other in the dress of a hermit. They were the first human beings the wanderers had met; and when Falkland gave the alarm to Riego, who slept beside him, it was immediately proposed to detain them as guides to the town of Carolina, where Riego had hopes of finding effectual assistance, or the means of ultimate escape. The hermit and his companion refused, with much vehemence, the office imposed upon them; but Riego ordered them to be forcibly detained. He had afterwards reason bitterly to regret this compulsion.

Midnight came on in all the gorgeous beauty of a southern heaven, and beneath its stars they renewed their march.

As Falkland rode by the side of Riego, the latter said to him in a low voice, "There is yet escape for you and my followers; none for me: they have set a price on my head, and the moment I leave these mountains, I enter upon my own destruction."

"No, Rafael!" replied Falkland; "you can yet fly to England, that asylum of the free, though ally of the despotic; the abettor of tyranny, but the shelter of its victims!" Riego answered, with the same faint and dejected tone, "I care not now what becomes of me! I have lived solely for Freedom; I have made her my mistress, my hope, my dream; I have no existence but in her. With the last effort of my country let me perish also! I have lived to view liberty not only defeated, but derided; I have seen its efforts not aided, but mocked. In my own country, those only who wore it have been respected who used it as a covering to ambition. In other nations, the free stood aloof when the charter of their own rights was violated in the invasion of ours. I cannot forget that the senate of that England, where you promise me a home, rang with insulting plaudits when her statesman breathed his ridicule on our weakness, not his sympathy for our cause; and I — *I*, — fanatic, dreamer, enthusiast, as I may be called, whose whole life has been one unremitting struggle for the opinion I have adopted — am at least not so blinded by my infatuation but I can see the mockery it incurs. If I die on the scaffold to-morrow, I shall have nothing of martyrdom but its doom; not the triumph, the incense, the immortality of popular applause: I should have no hope to support me at such a moment, gleaned from the glories of the future,—nothing but one stern and prophetic conviction of the vanity of that tyranny by which my sentence will be pronounced."

Riego paused for a moment before he resumed, and his pale and death-like countenance received an awful and unnatural light from the intensity of the feeling that swelled and burned within him. His figure was drawn up to its full height, and his voice rang through the lonely hills with a deep and hollow sound, that had in it a tone of prophecy, as he resumed: "It is in vain that they oppose OPINION; anything else they may subdue. They may conquer wind, water, nature itself; but to the progress of that secret, subtle, pervading spirit, their imagination can devise, their strength can accomplish, no bar: *its votaries* they may seize, they may destroy; *itself* they cannot touch. If they check it in one place, it invades them in another. They cannot build a wall across the whole earth; and, even if they could, it would pass over its summit! Chains cannot bind it,—for it is immaterial; dungeons enclose it,—for it is universal. Over the fagot and the scaffold, over the bleeding bodies of its defenders which they pile against its path, it sweeps on with a noiseless but unceasing march. Do they levy armies against it, it presents to them no palpable object to oppose. *Its camp is the universe; its asylum is the bosoms of their own soldiers.* Let them depopulate, destroy as they please, to each extremity of the earth; but as long as they have a single supporter themselves, as long as they leave a single individual into whom that spirit can enter, so long they will have the same labours to encounter, and the same enemy to subdue."

As Riego's voice ceased, Falkland gazed upon him with a mingled pity and admiration. Sour and ascetic as was the mind of that hopeless and disappointed man, he felt somewhat of a kindred glow at the pervading and holy enthusiasm of the patriot to whom he had listened; and though it was the character of his own philosophy to question the purity of human motives, and to smile at the more vivid emotions he had ceased to feel, he bowed his soul in homage to those principles whose sanctity he acknowledged, and to that devotion of zeal and fervour with which their defender cherished and enforced them. Falkland had joined the constitutionalists with respect, but not ardour, for their cause. He demanded excitation; he cared little where he found it. He stood in this world a being who mixed in all its changes, performed all its offices, took, as if by the force of superior mechanical power, a leading share in its events; but whose thoughts and soul were as offsprings of another planet, imprisoned in a human form, and *longing for their home!*

As they rode on, Riego continued to converse with that imprudent unreserve which the openness and warmth of his nature made natural to him; not one word escaped the hermit and the peasant (whose name was Lopez Lara) as they rode on two mules behind Falkland and Riego. "Remember," whispered the hermit to his comrade, "the reward!" "I do," muttered the peasant.

Throughout the whole of that long and dreary night, the wanderers rode on incessantly, and found themselves at daybreak near a farmhouse: this was Lara's own home. They made the peasant Lara knock; his own brother opened the door. Fearful as they were of the detection to which so numerous a party might conduce, only Riego, another officer (Don Luis de Sylva), and Falkland entered the house. The latter, whom nothing ever seemed to render weary or forgetful, fixed his cold stern eye upon the two brothers, and, seeing some signs pass between them, locked the door, and so prevented their escape. For a few hours they reposed in the stables with their horses, their drawn swords by their sides. On waking, Riego found it absolutely necessary that his horse should be shod. Lopez started up, and offered to lead it to Arguillas for that purpose.

"No," said Riego, who, though naturally imprudent, partook in this instance of Falkland's habitual caution: "your brother shall go and bring hither the farrier."

Accordingly the brother went: he soon returned. "The

farrier," he said, "was already on the road." Riego and his companions, who were absolutely fainting with hunger, sat down to breakfast; but Falkland, who had finished first, and who had eyed the man since his return with the most scrutinizing attention, withdrew towards the window, looking out from time to time with a telescope which they had carried about them, and urging them impatiently to finish.

"Why?" said Riego, "famished men are good for nothing, either to fight or fly — and we *must* wait for the farrier."

"True," said Falkland, "but —" he stopped abruptly. Sylva had his eyes on his face at that moment. Falkland's colour suddenly changed: he turned round with a loud cry. "Up! up! Riego! Sylva! We are undone,— the soldiers are upon us!"

"Arm!" cried Riego, starting up.

At that moment, Lopez and his brother seized their own carbines, and levelled them at the betrayed constitutionalists. "The first who moves," cried the former, "is a dead man!"

"Fools!" said Falkland, with a calm bitterness, advancing deliberately towards them. He moved only three steps,— Lopez fired. Falkland staggered a few paces, recovered himself, sprang towards Lara, clove him at one blow from the skull to the jaw, and fell, with his victim, lifeless upon the floor.

"Enough!" said Riego to the remaining peasant; "we are your prisoners; bind us!" In two minutes more the soldiers entered, and they were conducted to Carolina. Fortunately Falkland was known, when at Paris, to a French officer of high rank then at Carolina. He was removed to the Frenchman's quarters. Medical aid was instantly procured. The first examination of his wound was decisive; recovery was hopeless!

. . . .

Night came on again, with her pomp of light and shade,— the night that for Falkland had no morrow. One solitary lamp burned in the chamber where he lay alone with God and his own heart. He had desired his couch to be placed by the window and requested his attendants to withdraw. The gentle and balmy air stole over him, as free and bland as if it were to breathe for him forever; and the silver moonlight came gleaming through the lattice, and played upon his wan brow, like the tenderness of a bride that sought to kiss him to repose. "In a few hours," thought he, as he lay gazing on the high stars which seemed such silent witnesses of an eternal and unfathomed mystery,— "in a few hours either this feverish and wayward spirit will be at rest forever, or it will have commenced a new career in an untried and unimaginable existence! In a very few hours I may be amongst the very heavens that I survey,—a part of their own glory, a new link in a new order of beings, breathing amidst the elements of a more gorgeous world, arrayed myself in the attributes of a purer and diviner nature, a wanderer among the planets, an associate of angels, the beholder of the arcana of the great God,— redeemed, regenerate, immortal, or —*dust!*

"There is no Œdipus to solve the enigma of life. We are — whence came we? We are *not* — whither do we go? All things *in* our existence have their object: existence has none. We live, move, beget our species, perish — and *for what?* We ask the past its moral; we question the gone years of the reason of our being, and from the clouds of a thousand ages there goes forth no answer. Is it merely to pant beneath this weary load; to sicken of the sun; to grow old; to drop like leaves into the grave; and to bequeath to our heirs the worn garments of toil and labour that we leave behind? Is it to sail forever on the same sea, ploughing the ocean of time with new furrows, and feeding its billows with new wrecks, or — " and his thoughts paused, blinded and bewildered.

No man in whom the mind has not been broken by the decay of the body has approached death in full consciousness, as Falkland did that moment, and not thought intensely on the change he was about to undergo; and yet what new discoveries upon that subject has any one bequeathed us? There the wildest imaginations are driven from originality into triteness; there all minds — the frivolous and the strong, the busy and the idle — are compelled into the same path and limit of reflection. Upon that unknown and voiceless gulf of inquiry broods an eternal and impenetrable gloom; no wind breathes over it, no wave agitates its stillness: over the dead and solemn calm there is no change propitious to adventure; there goes forth no vessel of research, which is not driven, baffled and broken, again upon the shore.

The moon waxed high in her career. Midnight was gathering slowly over the earth; the beautiful, the mystic hour, blent with a thousand memories, hallowed by a thousand dreams, made tender to remembrance by the vows our youth breathed beneath its star, and solemn by the olden legends which are linked to its majesty and peace,—*the hour in which men should die;* the isthmus between two worlds; the climax of the past day; the verge of that which is to come; wrapping us in sleep after a weary travail, and promising us a morrow *which since the first birth of Creation has never failed.* As the minutes glided on, Falkland felt himself grow gradually weaker and weaker. The pain of his wound had ceased, but a deadly sickness gathered over his heart; the room reeled before his eyes, and the damp chill mounted from his feet up, —up to the breast in which the life-blood waxed dull and thick.

As the hand of the clock pointed *to the half-hour after midnight,* the attendants who waited in the adjoining room heard a faint cry. They rushed hastily into Falkland's chamber; they found him stretched half out of the bed. His hand was raised towards the opposite wall; it dropped gradually as they approached him; and his brow, which was at first stern and bent, softened, shade by shade, into his usual serenity. But the dim film gathered fast over his eye, and the last coldness upon his limbs. He strove to raise himself as if to speak; the effort failed, and he fell motionless on his face. They stood by the bed for some moments in silence; at length they raised him. Placed against his heart was an open locket of dark hair, which one hand still pressed convulsively. They looked upon his countenance—a single glance was sufficient; it was hushed, proud, passionless, the seal of Death was upon it.

THE END.

www.ingramcontent.com/pod-product-compliance
Lightning Source LLC
Chambersburg PA
CBHW030344310726
48979CB00001B/177

* 9 7 8 1 4 3 4 4 9 7 6 0 4 *